BRACE YOURSELF FOR A WILD RIDE

From the opening line to the last, HIT RADIO is a blast. It grabs you by the throat and hurtles you along to a climax so intense, it will take your breath away.

Hilarious. Violent. Touching. Sad. HIT RADIO is all of those and more. It's a frightening journey into the darkest dementia of human nature.

'A riveting tour de force'.

BOOKS BY DAVID ROBBINS

The Endworld Universe

The ENDWORLD Series
The WILDERNESS series
The WHITE APACHE series
The BLOOD FEUD series
A GIRL, THE END OF THE WORLD AND EVERYTHING

Horror:

PRANK NIGHT
SPOOK NIGHT
HELL-O-WEEN
THE WERELING
THE WRATH
SPECTRE

Novels:

HIT RADIO
BLOOD CULT

Westerns:

THUNDER VALLEY
RIDE TO VALOR
DIABLO
TOWN TAMERS
BADLANDERS
GUNS ON THE PRAIRIE

Other Series:

The ANGEL U series
DAVY CROCKETT

Nonfiction:

HEAVY TRAFFIC

HIT RADIO

BY

David Robbins

Published by Mad Hornet Publications
Printed in the United States of America

ISBN 978-0-9839882-0-5

www.davidrobbinsauthor.com

MAD HORNET
PUBLISHING

Dedicated to Judy, Joshua and Shane

Now that it matters, but these events
take place in 1985.

CHAPTER ONE

Arty Johnson knew better but he was trying to impress a bodacious babe. He had the hots for a vixen in pink shorts and his brain had taken a back seat to his hormones.

Arty had just won big at roulette. The kind of big where his mouth went dry and his heart raced and he thought to himself, 'I must be dreaming.' But then, thanks to too many vodka gimlets, Arty prepared to bet the whole wad, every last dollar, on the next spin.

So nervous he could hardly stand still but trying to act cool, Arty glanced at Sugarpie, at those humongous boobs of hers. He loved how they jiggled, and she was a great jiggler. He thought of how he'd bragged on himself all night, how here was his chance to show her what he was made of.

The roulette man had seen it all before. Enough times that if he had ten bucks for all the suckers who let their lust get the better of their common sense, he would own *The Golden Nugget*. He spun the wheel and called out the winning number.

It wasn't the number Arty picked. He wanted to beat his head on the table. Or better yet, beat Sugarpie's. Instead, he swore under his breath as his winnings were raked in. More money than he'd won at one time, ever, gone in the blink of an eye. Taking Sugarpie's hand, he started to stand.

"Are you going to let them get away with that, Arty, baby?" she asked.

Arty stared at Sugarpie through an alcohol haze. Either she was swaying or he was. No, he didn't want to let the casino take his winnings but what could he do?

"I mean, if it was me, I'd keep on playing." Sugarpie jiggled some more and ran a red fingernail across the back of his hand.

Arty felt his cheeks grow hot. He slowly sat back down and tried to get his brain to work, which was difficult to do with what sounded like water sloshing around in his skull. "Will you take a marker?" he heard himself ask, his thick tongue wagging of its own accord.

The roulette operator signaled the floorman.

Before Arty knew it, a guy in a dark suit was at his side. The man leaned over to confer. Ronco, he said his name was. Arty answered some questions, bobbed his chin a few times.

Ronco stepped to a special phone over on the wall and reported to someone higher up. He talked a long time. When he came back he was smiling.

For some reason that smile reminded Arty of the stuffed barracuda his brother had in his den.

"Good news, Mr. Johnson. Your marker is good for two hundred thousand."

Arty's jaw nearly dropped. He didn't have much more than a couple grand in the bank. His house wouldn't be paid off until he was old enough to collect social security. And he always drove a leaser so he could write it off as a business expense. His total assets, in short, were next to zip. Someone had made a mistake. Arty didn't let on. He played it smart. Sitting up straight, he wagged a finger at the roulette wheel. 'Let's try that again.'

Sugarpie giggled. She was a great giggler, too. Every

time she did, her jugs jiggled. It was distracting.

Eleven minutes. That was all it took. Arty Johnson lost the full two hundred thousand and was sitting there with his head in his hands and tears in his eyes when strong hands fell on his shoulders and two huskies pried him from his seat and steered him toward a far door. Ronco led the way.

Arty didn't resist or protest. He assumed they were taking him to see their boss. There would be papers to sign and he'd be given a long lecture on how he must meet his payments on time. Then they'd send him on his way.

It wasn't like the old days when the Mafia ran Las Vegas, when a guy had to worry about having his arms and legs broken, or worse. The government had seen to that. The Feds had driven the Mob out of Vegas. Hell, clear out of Nevada.

The politicians and the press like to crow that Las Vegas and Reno and the rest were as clean as a nun's habit. Some of the politicians knew better but the press parroted their claims.

The Mafia had done what it always did whenever the heat was on. It adapted, it adjusted, it survived. It always survived. And it thrived.

On the books, the public books, *The Golden Nugget* was a legitimate concern. But the man who supposedly ran the casino didn't actually run it. The president of the corporation, the front man, was in fact an underling. The real owner, the real boss, was Franco 'Big Frank' Scarvetti. It was one of the best-kept secrets in Vegas, strictly a need-to-know basis, and only wiseguys and a few select others had the need.

As the elevator bore Arty Johnson up, he wrung his hands and gnawed on his lip like a schoolboy about to be hauled before the principal for misbehaving.

The elevator stopped and hissed open and Arty saw two more bruisers on either side of a mahogany door. One nodded at Ronco and opened it and Arty trailed Ronco in.

The room was lavish, with plush carpet thick enough to dive into. Other than that, it was no different from any other executive office, with a desk and chairs and a sofa along one wall. Arty had no reason to be alarmed. He sank into the chair Ronco steered him to and smiled sheepishly at the big man who sat behind the desk.

"I guess I am in deep now," Arty joked.

"Yes, you are."

Arty stiffened. The man had replied without batting an eye in a voice that reminded Arty of gravel grating on metal. His sluggish brain flared to life and he noticed things he hadn't noticed before. Little things. Like how big the guy really was. Big and broad and massive as a wall. And how the man's dark eyes bored into his like twin drills. "I beg your pardon?"

"You heard me, Mr. Johnson."

Arty felt queasy. Something was wrong but he couldn't put his finger on it. "I'm good for the money, Mr.---"

Franco Scarvetti had no intention of revealing who he was just yet. He studied the man who might be the solution to a problem he had. He noted the cheap suit, the cheap cologne. No class, he decided. And no balls? That was the important question. Big Frank felt he knew the answer. Because if there was one thing that growing up on the mean streets of the Windy City had taught him, it was how to read people. How to tell the sheep from the wolves. This was no wolf.

Arty Johnson took to squirming like he had fleas in his polka-dot boxers. "Is there a problem?"

"You tell me," Big Frank said. "You're the one who went out on a limb for two hundred grand. How do you expect to make good?"

"Installments. Isn't that how it's done? Tell me how much to pay each month and I'll make the payments. Honest."

"Do you really expect us to wait twenty years?" Big Frank gruffly demanded. "You must mistake us for a bank. No, I'm afraid the money is due when we say it's due. And it's due now."

Arty blanched. "How's that again?"

"You heard me. I'm calling in your marker, Mr. Johnson," Big Frank informed him. "My prerogative."

Stunned, Arty said, "I'm not sure I understand."

"Sure you do. Pay up or pay the piper. That's how this works."

"You must be kidding." Arty couldn't believe what he was hearing. The casino couldn't demand the money like this. It wasn't right. It wasn't legal, or at least he hoped it wasn't. He shook his head to clear it but his mind wouldn't work.

Ordinarily, Big Frank tolerated only so much stupidity. But he decided to be patient. This mark's whole world was about to come crashing down and Big Frank didn't want the guy to go off the deep end. Not yet. Not before the papers were signed and notarized. "Would you like a cup of coffee, Mr. Johnson?"

"Would I!" Arty gratefully exclaimed. "Yes, please. Cream and sugar, if you don't mind." He wanted more than that. He wanted to pinch himself and wake up. He tried it, pinching his wrist until it hurt, but the room and the men in the dark suits and the big one across the desk were still there. It was real. All too horribly real.

Big Frank motioned at Ronco who picked up one of several phones while Big Frank continued to study the answer to his dilemma. Fate had delivered a godsend. It could buy him the time he needed to set things right, to cool tempers, to save his only son.

There were four things in the world Big Frank cared about. Foremost was the casino. Thirty years of his life had gone into making *The Golden Nugget* a success and he would sooner part with a vital organ than see it fail. Then came his son, his daughter, and his wife, in that order.

Louis Scarvetti was Big Frank's heir. It was Little Lou who would one day step into Big Frank's shoes when he stepped down. Big Frank could still remember how wonderful it felt to hold the squealing newborn in his arms. He could still recall the tingle that shot down his spine at the thought that one day the empire he was carving out would belong to his own flesh and blood.

Big Frank scowled. How could he have foreseen all the headaches and heartaches Little Lou would cause? Some boys were born to trouble. It was his sad lot in life to have a son who drew it like a rotting corpse drew flies. The most recent incident was the latest in a long string. But it was the most serious, with a consequence Big Frank was determined to spare his son from, whatever it took.

Arty Johnson was wringing his hands. He didn't like how the big guy kept staring. Now that he had a few moments to think, he realized he was letting himself be intimidated for no reason. No matter what the big man said, the casino couldn't make him fork over money he didn't have. They were trying to scare him, was all. Well, it wouldn't work. He'd play along with their game for the time being. Then, when he was safely back in Yuba City, he'd thumb his nose at them and let his lawyer haggle it out. It was about damn time that Skimmer Hamilton earned his retainer.

The crafty gleam that came into Arty's eyes wasn't lost on Big Frank. The worm thinks it can turn, he reflected, and he smiled.

It was a smile so cold, so chilling, that Arty Johnson's breath caught in his throat. He nearly leaped out of his chair when the door opened to admit another husky bearing a tray. The aroma of coffee soothed him somewhat. Arty was profoundly grateful when Ronco poured a cup for him but he was embarrassed his hands shook when he accepted it.

Big Frank waited until Johnson had taken several sips. "Now then, down to business. You owe us two hundred thou. We want the money or we want its equivalent."

"Equivalent?" Arty repeated, confused. Fidgeting in his chair, he said, "Look here, whoever you are. You can't be serious. I mean, I don't carry that much around on me." He was thinking as fast as he could. Warmed by the coffee, he was feeling halfway himself again although his head was still filled with cobwebs. "It will take me a while to liquidate some stock and sell off a few others assets but I can assure you that you'll---."

Big Frank held up a hand. "Don't."

"Excuse me?"

"Don't insult my intelligence."

Arty balanced the saucer on his leg. He was growing mad. Who did this joker think he was, acting so high and mighty? "I don't know what you're talking about, friend," he said glibly. He'd show this big goon. Back in his days in sales, he'd been able to charm an Adventist into advertising on *The Catholic Hour*. Talking his way out of this fix should be child's play. "First thing in the morning I'll put a call through to my broker and my banker and get the ball rolling. You'll have your dough by the end of the month at the latest, I promise."

"I warned you, Mr. Johnson." Big Frank picked up a phone and stabbed a button. "Tell the Iceman I need him. And ring downstairs for a bucket of ice and a finger splint."

CHAPTER TWO

Arty Johnson froze in the act of raising his cup. What the hell was that about? he almost asked.

A door at the rear opened and in sauntered a tall man whose wavy shock of black hair was matched by a black suit and black shoes.

Arty snickered. He couldn't help it. The man made him think of that movie, *Men in Black*. The man even wore sunglasses, the kind with mirror lenses. Aviator shades, he thought they were called.

"This is Mr. Johnson," Big Frank said, nodding at Arty. "Break the little finger on his left hand."

Shocked, Arty sat there and watched the man in black come toward him. The guy moved like a cat, with no wasted motion. Not uttering a word, the man gripped Arty's left wrist in one hand and Arty's little finger in the other. The contact galvanized Arty to life. "Now wait just a damned minute."

There was a loud crack.

It happened so fast, Arty's finger was broken and dangling before his brain registered the pain. He heaved erect, spilling hot coffee on his pants.

The Iceman twisted Arty's wrist and slammed him back down as easily as Arty would handle a six-year old.

Arty opened his mouth to cry out but the Iceman clamped a hand over it, stifling his screech. In vain Arty clawed at the Iceman's fingers. They were steel. Arty had never known anyone so strong.

"Listen up, Mr. Johnson," Big Frank said quietly. "I want you to compose yourself. I want you to sit there and listen and I'll tell you how things are and how they're going to be. We'll tend to your finger. We'll take care of all your needs from here on out. But if you lie to me again, if you treat me with disrespect, I'll have the Iceman stick an icepick in your balls. Do you understand?"

The Iceman removed his hand from Arty's mouth and stepped back.

All Arty could do was gape. He was stunned to his core, positively speechless. Over and over in his head the same refrain repeated itself. 'This can't be happening. This can't be happening. This can't be happening.'

Big Frank wasn't in any hurry. He would take all night if need be. Every angle had to be worked out. When the ice and split were brought in, he had Ronco set the finger. All the while, Arty Johnson of Yuba City had a look of dumb amazement on his face. Under other circumstances it would have been comical. But Big Frank had too much at stake to laugh at the schmuck's expense.

Arty was numb, numb in mind as well as his body. He watched his finger being taped with an air of detachment that astonished him almost as much as having it broken. It was as if he were someone else. When the job was done, he mumbled, "Thank you."

"Take off your pants," Big Frank said.

Seized by panic, Arty glanced up. "What in the world are you talking about?"

"We need to have them cleaned before the stains set in."

"Stains?" Arty said, then remembered spilling his

coffee. "Oh. That. There's no need to bother. Don't put yourself out on my account."

"Take them off."

What do you say to someone who has just had your finger broken like a dry twig? Arty fumbled at his belt buckle, and had to be helped. He was relieved to see that the Iceman had taken a seat on the sofa and was reading a magazine, *Popular Mechanics*.

One of the huskies whisked out with Arty's trousers.

Standing there in his polka-dot boxers, Arty felt exposed and helpless. These men could kill him and there was nothing he could do to stop them. He was a bug waiting to be squashed underfoot.

"Sit," Big Frank said.

Arty sat.

Big Frank picked up the phone, punched another button. "I'm ready for Eddy the Book."

Through a different door on the far side of the room came a squat man carrying an accountant's ledger, of all things. Except for tufts over each ear, his hair had given up the ghost. Momentarily visible behind him were computers manned by smartly dressed personnel.

"Give me the rundown for him to hear," Big Frank said.

Eddy the Book consulted the ledger and read off, "Name, Artemis Turley Johnson. Father, deceased. Mother is in a nursing home. He lives at 101 Durian Court, Yuba City, Nevada. His wife's name is Meriam. They've been married sixteen years and have two kids. A boy, Artemis Junior, age nine, and a girl, Lucille, who's five."

"How in the world?" Arty marveled.

"Get to the money," Big Frank directed.

Eddy the Book ran his finger down a page. "They have a joint checking account at First National of Yuba City. Current balance is two thousand, four hundred and sixty-five dollars and forty-nine cents."

When Eddy the Book didn't go on, Big Frank looked up. "That's it? No savings? No IRA's? Securities? Bonds?"

"None whatsoever. What with their house and the station, they're in hock up to their armpits."

Everyone except the Iceman stared at Arty as if he were guilty of a crime. He wished he could shrivel into his chair. He started to fidget but the feel of his boxers on his bottom stopped him. He didn't want to give these men wicked ideas. "How do you know so much?"

Big Frank sighed. It never ceased to surprise him, how far simpletons could go in life. "I have Eddy, here to thank. He's real big on technology. He says we're into something called the Information Age. And information, Mr. Johnson, is power. For instance, you booked your room using one of your credit cards, correct?" Of course it was correct but Big Frank was making small talk to put the mark at ease.

Arty bobbed his chin.

"With that we ran a credit check on you. We also have sources in the banking industry and government. Anything we need to find out, we usually can. Information no one else can get on short notice."

"It sounds like something the C.I.A. would do," Arty said. "Spying on folks."

"It's not spying so much as protecting ourselves. We can't have people taking advantage of us, now can we?"

"I suppose not," Arty begrudgingly agreed.

"Now you see why I was angry with you," Big Frank said.

"I knew you didn't have the money to cover your marker. Never try to scam a scam artist or you'll take it on the chin every time."

"Or the finger," Arty said.

Big Frank laughed. "I'm starting to like you, Mr. Johnson. A sense of humor comes in handy. Don't lose yours and you'll get through this a lot better off." To Eddy the Book he said, "Give me what counts."

"It's a fifty-thousand watt FM. Gross revenue last year was two hundred and sixty-three grand. Sounds like a lot but when you deduct salaries and expense they were lucky to stay afloat."

"Break it down."

"Wunderkund here pocketed thirty big ones. He pays his engineer twenty-five thousand. Two salesmen, salaries and commissions combined, total forty-two. Announcers and a program director, ninety-four. A secretary, eighteen. Operating expenses, twenty-seven. " Eddy paused. "Plus there are the bank payments. Two grand a month."

Big Frank did the math in his head. "They cleared a measly three g's?"

"Three thousand, one hundred and forty-nine dollars and seventy-six cents."

Arty sipped a fresh cup of coffee handed to him by Ronco. He didn't understand all this interest in his radio station. Then it hit him. They must have intended to cut themselves in for a percentage of the profits. Well, the joke was on them because as they'd just learned, there wasn't enough profit to make it worth their while.

"It will have to do," Big Frank remarked. "Get everything together. You're going with them."

Eddy the Book did a double-take. "Me? I'm not part of

his crew. What good would I be?"

"You're to go over the books at the other end. Sit in on the meetings between the attorneys. Make sure there are no snags with the sale. Then, and only then, report back to me."

Arty's interest perked. "What was that about a sale?" he made bold to ask. They couldn't possibly mean what he suspected they meant.

Big Frank had to break the news sometime and it might as well be now, while the guy was missing his pants and less likely to do something stupid. "You owe two hundred thousand, Mr. Johnson. Since you don't have the money, I'm taking your radio station in payment. On paper it will appear as if you sold it to me for that amount. You get to stay on as vice-president in charge of marketing with the same salary you were making before."

"You're joking."

"Do I look like I am?"

It was the last straw. Arty had been humiliated. He'd been brutally savaged. His left hand throbbed with agony, his legs were bare to the world, and now his livelihood was being stripped from him. He grew hot with outrage and started to stand.

"Don't," Big Frank said.

Arty froze.

"Do you really want to have the Iceman come back over here?"

Gulping, Arty glanced at the man in the sunglasses, who had traded the *Popular Mechanics* for a *Gun World*. He eased down into his chair.

No balls at all, Big Frank thought happily. The change in ownership promised to go smoothly. He had what he so desperately needed.

Turning to Ronco, Big Frank said, "Get hold of Lou. I want him and his entire crew here within the hour."

"Yes, sir, Mr. Scarvetti."

Arty Johnson cleared his throat and said sorrowfully, "I've sure stepped in it, haven't I?"

"You sure as hell have," Big Frank said, and made a mental note to see that Sugarpie got a bonus for her performance.

CHAPTER THREE

Louis Alfonse Scarvetti and his crew arrived at the *Golden Nugget* fifty-five minutes later. They didn't go straight to the elevators. Lou strutted in among the slots and the tables to nod and smile at dealers and floormen and ogle women. He liked to think of the casino as his even though it wouldn't be until his father was ready to step down, which could be a good many years yet.

His nickname was Little Lou. Not because he was Big Frank's son but because in his bare feet he barely reached five feet. His height was a sore spot with him. The last person to poke fun at it, a gambler in a high stakes game, lost most of his front teeth.

Behind his back everyone called Little Lou by another nickname: Cry Baby. He earned it thanks to a bad habit he picked up when he was still toddling in *Huggies*. Whenever things didn't go his way, Lou ran to daddy. If his mother gave him a hard time, he whined about how mean she was. If a nanny dared discipline him, Lou threw a screaming fit. Any time Lou's feelings were hurt, he complained or cried or both.

Little Lou stopped crying when he was fourteen but by then he was Cry Baby to everyone except Big Frank. No one could remember who coined it but it stuck.

The past few years, Cry Baby hadn't run to his father as often. He preferred to handle his problems on his own. Unfortunately, his idea of how to deal with them was to eliminate them by any means necessary.

It didn't help matters that Cry Baby had a temper. He was notorious for going ballistic, and the person he was mad at better watch out. If anyone gave him lip, they ate theirs. If anyone stood up to him, he had his crew teach them why they shouldn't. The *Nugget* staff lived in fear of him. It wa so bad, the maids flipped a coin each day to see who had to clean his suite.

Cry Baby imagined himself as a world-class tough guy like the gangsters in the movies he loved to watch.

One of his fondest memories was of the time a smartass busboy mouthed off to him when Cry Baby carped about a table not being clean. Cry Baby went at the kid with a butter knife and jammed it into his throat. Fortunately, they were in a private dining room only the Family used. There were no witnesses other than Cry Baby's crew, and they buried the body in the desert.

When Big Frank found out, he gave Cry Baby a talking to.

Big Frank was well liked. Everyone knew where they stood with him. He expected the best from his people and in return he treated them fairly. So long as they did their job to the best of their ability, they were okay. Even if they occasionally screwed up, if it was an honest mistake, Big Frank forgave them. But do something stupid, cause Big Frank aggravation, and the culprit was in a world of hurt.

With one exception.

Cry Baby got away with murder. Time and again he ended up in trouble. Time and again Big Frank bailed him out. On the few occasions when Big Frank punished him, the punishments were laughable.

Cry Baby was Big Frank's weak spot, his Achilles' heel.

Big Frank overlooked anything his son did. Anything. Then took whatever steps were needed to protect Cry Baby.

It had gotten to the point where Cry Baby thought he was invincible. He could whack someone and not break a sweat knowing his father would see to it that the bodies were disposed of, the witnesses were silenced, and juries were bought off.

Or, rather, the crew that Big Frank had hand-picked for Cry Baby saw to all that. They had one trait in common, this crew. They were loyal to a fault. Loyal to Big Frank, not to Cry Baby.

The first wiseguy Big Frank tabbed was Pretty Boy. Angelo Tepia was his given name but no one used given names much. Pretty Boy had a love affair with mirrors. The other wiseguys liked to joke that he'd marry one if he could. Every polished surface he walked past, he checked out his reflection. He was so in love with himself, the line went, that he went through withdrawal if he couldn't see his shadow.

Dill was next to be chosen. His thing was pickles. He was addicted, and always carried a jar around in his pocket. Dill pickles, not the sweet. Rumor had it he sliced a few up each morning and put them on his cereal. He also had a pickle for a brain, as Cry Baby phrased it, but he was built like a gorilla and could bench press three hundred and fifty. When bones had to be busted, Dill was the man to do the busting.

The Wolfman was the quiet one. His 'condition', as he called it, was to blame. He was as hairy as his namesake. So hairy, people stared when he was in public. Even his nose hairs had hairs, the others liked to joke. He shaved twice a day but it didn't help. Half an hour later he had hairs sprout all over. When he was growing up he was teased a lot, called a freak and a misfit, and it left scars. He withdrew into himself. But he was a good soldier and practically worshipped Big Frank.

The same was true of Switch. He was the only blond on the crew, the only button man who wore his hair in a buzz cut, and the only soldier who favored knives over a gun. He was a virtuoso with switchblades, fancy Italian jobs with ivory handles. When he wasn't sharpening them he was throwing them. He practiced hour after hour, day after day, constantly honing his skill.

Valentino was the last wiseguy Big Frank chose. He was the youngest. He was by far the handsomest, as well, Pretty Boy nothwithstanding. Valentino was into foxy ladies and foxy ladies were into him. He had a different showgirl on his arm every night. Incredibly enough, he was such sheer eye candy, so charming and so sexy in a sensual young-Al-Pacino kind of way, he'd never met a woman who turned him down.

Among the other crews, Cry Baby's was known as 'the Losers'. Not that they were incompetent. Quite the opposite. They were five of the best soldiers in the Scarvetti organization. They were called the Losers simply because they were Cry Baby's men.

On this particular night, Cry Baby finally tired of strutting and led them to the bank of elevators.

Only Cry Baby, Valentino and Switch were admitted to Big Frank's office. The rest had to wait in the hall.

Cry Baby took three steps and stopped. His father and one other were present. It was the man in the Aviators, reading on the sofa, who brought him up short. "Iceman," he said curtly.

The Iceman flipped a page in a *Sports Illustrated* swimsuit edition. He looked up but he didn't return the greeting. He didn't even acknowledge Cry Baby existed.

Coming from anyone else, it would be the ultimate insult. Cry Baby would throw a fit. Valentino and Switch saw him flush and clench his fists but he didn't say anything.

The chief enforcer was the one person who was immune to Cry Baby's tantrums.

All any of the wiseguys knew about the Iceman was that he'd been Big Frank's personal lethal weapon since Big Frank's days in Chi Town. His real identity, everything about his past, were shrouded in mystery. It was claimed he came from the same rough and vicious neighborhood as Big Frank, that he'd made his bones when he was still a teen, and that the first person he killed was a member of his family.

One other thing was known about the Iceman. He had a very special talent. He could whack anyone or anything, anywhere, at any time. He could take a cute little kitten or a cuddly little puppy and wring its neck.

Once a month he did just that.

Big Frank would have a soldier answer a newspaper ad for a free pet or go to the animal shelter and pick out the most adorable kitten or puppy. And the Iceman would kill it. All the wiseguys wanted to know why.

One of them found out.

CHAPTER FOUR

Three months earlier.

Valentino's turn came. He'd returned from the animal shelter with a cocker spaniel pup with loving eyes and a moist nose and brought it to the Iceman's room at the casino. His knuckles barely touched the door when it opened.

Val reined in his nerves and held out the puppy. "Here you go," he said. "No one told me if you like extra cheese and pepperoni so I got you one plain."

"Was that a joke" the Iceman asked.

"Yeah."

"It's a good thing you don't do stand-up." The Iceman took the cocker spaniel and went to shut the door.

Val took a gamble. This was the most the Iceman ever said to him. Hell, it was the most he'd ever heard the Iceman say to anyone except Big Frank. "Mind if I ask you a question?"

The Iceman had looked at him with those spooky tinted Aviators. Finally he said, "What?"

No one was supposed to talk to the Iceman when they dropped off an animal. They were to hand it over and go. But Val couldn't resist. His curiosity was too great. "Why do you do this? I mean, what purpose does it serve?"

"You said one question. That was two. You count as good as you do stand-up."

Val couldn't believe it. The Iceman had made a joke.

He laughed to be polite. Then the Iceman shocked him by motioning for him to enter.

The suite was nice. Not outstanding like Big Frank's, but nice. Crossing to an easy chair, the Iceman sat with the pup in his lap and commenced to stroke it. The cocker spaniel licked his fingers.

Val waited. He stood as still as a petrified tree and hoped his face didn't betray how nervous he was.

Apparently the Iceman could read minds. "Relax. I'm not so hardass I'd off you for breaking the rules."

"Then why do this?" Val said. "The hits I can understand." He nodded at the puppy. "This I can't. It's not like you have anything to prove. The Petrello hit alone, nine guys you wasted. Nine!" He didn't try to hide his admiration. "Yet you kill puppies and kittens."

The Aviators locked on him and for seconds that were eternities the Iceman didn't speak.

Val was afraid that he'd overstepped himself and come morning the rest of the crew would cart his remains out to the desert.

"How many men have you whacked, Valentino?"

Val hesitated. Wiseguys never asked that question. It was impolite. Not to mention dangerous. The fewer who knew, the safer for the soldier. But that wasn't why he hesitated. He was ashamed to admit the truth. "None."

The enforcer's eyebrows arched above his sunglasses. "You don't say? I was under the impression you're a made man."

"Big Frank treats me like one," Val said. "He says that as far as he's concerned, I am."

"Franco must like you."

"What makes you say that?"

The Iceman continued to stroke the puppy and scratch behind its long floppy ears. "Wiseguys have to earn their buttons. Until they do, no matter how well connected they are, they aren't made men. Franco is treating you as if you are when technically you don't deserve the honor." The Iceman paused, and frowned. "But then, he always protects those he cares for."

Val wondered if the Iceman was referring to Cry Baby. "What is he protecting me from?"

"Yourself."

That made no sense that Val could see. He pointed at the cocker spaniel, which was lathering the Iceman's hand in an excess of misguided canine devotion. "You're really going to go through with it? After you've held him and petted him?"

Instead of answering, the Iceman asked a question of his own. "Since you've never whacked a man, can I take it you've never whacked a woman, either?"

"No, and I hope to God I never have to."

"I've had to," the Iceman said. "Most I've shot. It's over fast and there's not much pain." He rubbed under the puppy's chin and it was in heaven. "A few I've strangled. The ones who didn't deserve the mercy of a bullet."

Val didn't want to hear this. He truly didn't.

"Then there was the wife of that capo, Finelli. It was before your time. She was cheating on him with a police captain. The cop only wanted to milk her for information but she was too dumb to realize she was being used." The Iceman patted the spaniel's head and it wagged its tail in delight. "Franco sat down with Finelli and they had a heart-to-heart. The result was that I had to chop Mrs. Finelli into bits and pieces, and her husband used them for fish bait on an outing to Lake Tahoe."

Val wondered why the chief enforcer was telling him this. It could earn the Iceman the chair. Was he that confident in the fear he inspired?

"Have you ever killed a child?"

"Hell, no. Who would want to?" Val said without thinking, and regretted it when the Iceman's lips pinched together.

"Let's say there are witnesses to a snuff job, a family, maybe, who can put one of us behind bars for life. Do you let them live and our guy takes a fall? Or do you ensure they don't pose a threat to you and yours?"

"I'd hate to have to make a decision like that."

"Franco has to make them all the time. And when he decides it's in our best interests to silence someone, no matter if they're male or female or how young or old, he needs someone who can do the job. Could you?"

"You know I can't."

"How about Switch? Or Pretty Boy? Or the Wolfman?"

Val had to admit none of them were capable of icing a child, so far as he knew. "But there's always Cry Baby," he added, only partly in jest. "He'd waste his own brother if he had one."

The Iceman's features grew hard as flint. "Ah, yes. Louis. He's a rare breed, I agree. But a mad dog on a leash is still a mad dog."

Everyone was aware that Cry Baby and the Iceman didn't get along. But what Val heard in the Iceman's voice that day was pure and total hate. For the enforcer to show so much emotion was unsettling.

The Iceman was silent a bit, then went calmly on. "It's always hard whacking a child. You can't dwell on it, you can't think about it in advance or while you're doing it. You just do it and when you're done, you hope you don't puke your guts out."

This was a whole new side to the enforcer, one Val wasn't sure how to relate to.

"A guy in a magazine once wrote that it's easier to destroy than to create. That's bullshit. To kill another human being is one of the hardest things we can do. It takes guts. It takes will. When the target is a kid, it takes all you have inside. Just like it does to wring the neck of a kitten or a puppy."

And with that, the Iceman gave a powerful wrench and the cocker spaniel's neck snapped with a loud crack.

It caught Val off-guard. He hadn't expected the Iceman to do it while he was there. "Jesus!" he blurted.

The puppy collapsed, its head at an unnatural angle.

"Killing is a skill," the Iceman said, continuing to pet the dead dog. "It must be maintained like any other skill. The more you practice, the better you are."

Somehow Val was able to say, "So you're telling me that you whack puppies and kittens to keep in practice?"

The incredible occurred: the Iceman took off his shades.

Val was privileged to see what none of the other wiseguys ever had. He saw the Iceman's eyes. Some of the soldiers were of the opinion they must be red like the eyes of a demon. Pretty Boy once remarked that the Iceman probably didn't have any, that behind the Aviator's were black holes like in that movie about angels. Dill thought they might be the kind of eyes a snake had. But they were entirely human, grey with floating flecks, like specks of metal adrift in liquid mercury. Staring into them rattled

Val more than staring at the one-way shades.

"I'm no different than a hunter who sights in his rifle before deer season or a fisherman who practices his casting in his driveway before a tournament."

Val had his failings, like everyone else. One of his was that he always told things like they were. "Come on," he then said. "Shooting at a target isn't the same as what you just did." He gestured at the lifeless husk. "I understand, though. It must be rough. I could never do your job. I'd have nightmares for the rest of my life."

"Each of us does what he must."

Again Val replied without thinking. "I feel sorry for you, Iceman. I really do."

The Iceman had slipped his Aviators back on. "I don't want your pity." His tone was as brittle as an egg shell.

"Who said anything about pity? I feel sorry, yeah, but sorry as in sympathy. As in I wouldn't be in your shoes for all the gold in Fort Knox." Val turned to go. "I didn't mean to bother you. Hope you won't hold it against me." At the door he glanced back. The Iceman was rubbing the dead puppy's ear. "There has to be an easier way."

"There isn't."

"Thanks for the talk. If you ever want to go have a drink or maybe catch a show, let me know." Val didn't know what made him say that last bit. The chief enforcer never hung out with the other wiseguys.

"You should go now."

Val went.

CHAPTER FIVE

Cry Baby plopped into a chair, crossed his legs, and broke out a pack of smokes. "I got your message, pops. What's so important I had to be dragged away from my old lady's watermelons?"

Val and Switch hung back near the door to show they had no interest in overhearing the conversation. Not that they could help it.

"It's this Scola business, Lou," Big Frank said. "I warned you not to let him get to you. But you wouldn't listen. You had to show him. You had to take a crowbar to his head."

"Fucking-A I did," Cry Baby said. "The bastard wouldn't stop bad-mouthing me. He told everybody and their grandmother what a lame wuss I am. Luigi, the fucking doorman, told me that Scola told him I was as worthless as they come. The son of a bitch was asking for it and I gave it to him."

Big Frank was displeased, and it showed. "We've been all through this. Scola was a made man. He had close ties to the Gambioso Family, and now they're demanding justice be done. They've asked for a sit-down. All the heads of the Families are to meet in Denver to talk over what is to be done with you."

"What the fuck is there to talk about?" Cry Baby bristled. "Just because Scola had his button doesn't mean he had the right to treat me like dirt. The prick had it in for me ever since I gave him a piece of my mind that time in Atlanta. Well, I showed him."

Big Frank turned to the window and pretended to be interested in the Las Vegas skyline. He'd done the best he could raising his son but it hadn't been good enough. Deep down, he'd always known he was too soft, that he let the apple of his eye do things that earned everyone else a dirt nap.

Big Frank blamed Dr. Spock. When Lou was still a toddler, his wife had gone on and on about how the good doctor's books were infallible guides to child-rearing. Big Frank let her have her way even though he thought the good doctor was full of it.

"Give the boy his space," Maria constantly criticized. "Remember how your father treated you, and how bitter you were? Do you want to make the same mistake? Treat Lou with respect. Nurture him, like Dr. Spock says. Feed his sensitive side and it will blossom and bloom like a rose."

A rose, hell, Big Frank reflected. He would have been smarter to listen to his grandfather.

"Spare the rod and spoil the brat," the old man liked to say. "That's in the Bible. I beat the hell out of your father every day of the week and twice on Sundays , and look at how he turned out. He hasn't sassed me once in seventy-eight years."

Cry Baby brought an end to Big Frank's reverie by saying, "Let me go to Denver with you. I'll tell those lame fucks how it was. How I went to Benny's Bar and Grill for a drink. How I was minding my own business until Scola came in. It was Scola who started it. Calling me names, saying I was chickenshit. That I have a pecker the size of a match. That sort of stuff." Cry Baby spread his hands. "What else was I to do? I waited for him to leave and jacked his sorry ass."

"Sticks and stones, son," Big Frank said. ""You still don't get it, do you? You don't' realize how deadly serious this is. You can't whack a made man without permission. It's not done. The Gambioso Family would be within their rights to put out a contract on you."

Cry Baby snickered. "Let them try and hit me. I dare them. I'll hit them right back, teach those sorry fucks to mess with me."

Big Frank came out of his chair so swiftly, he was around his desk and on Cry Baby before Cry Baby could blink. He seized his son by the shirt and hauled him to his feet. Cry Baby's hand rose toward his jacket.

The Iceman came off the sofa in a blur. He was at Cry Baby's side in two lightning strides.

For a few moments the tableau froze. Then Big Frank let go of his son and stepped back. Sinking onto the edge of his desk, he stared forlornly at the floor. His hands rose to his temples. "What have I done?" he asked no one in particular.

Cry Baby smoothed his shirt. "Get a fucking grip, pops. No one is going to fucking whack me. I can fucking take care of myself."

Valentino and Switch swapped glances. They'd never seen Big Frank look so sad.

"That's another thing, Lou," Big Frank said quietly. "Your mouth. How many times have I asked you not to talk like you were raised in the gutter? You even do it in front of your mother." Big Frank shook his head. "I know where you get it from. It's those Mafia movies you watch, and that TV show where they use the f-word nine times in a ten word sentence. Hollywood nonsense. No one talks like that in real life."

"Maybe you don't," Cry Baby said sullenly.

The Iceman was still standing near him, his features, as always, inscrutable.

Unexpectedly, Cry Baby turned and snarled, "What's your problem, badass? You'd love to whack me, wouldn't you? Why don't you go read your stupid magazines and let us real men have a private talk?"

To the amazement of both Val and Switch, the Iceman walked back to the sofa.

"Is this all, pops?" Cry Baby asked. "Because if you're done reaming me over that douche Victor Scola, I have things I could be doing."

Big Frank walked around the desk and sat. A change had come over him, an air of great regret. "No. There's more. I want to get you out of town until this blows over."

"Oh, yeah? Where to? Atlantic City? New York? Or how about Miami? I wouldn't mind lying in the sun and making it with babes in bikinis."

"You're going to Yuba City," Big Frank said.

"Isn't that off in the sticks somewhere? Why the fuck are you sending me there?"

"Because that's where the radio station is."

"What fucking radio station?"

"The one you're going to run."

CHAPTER SIX

"Keep a low profile," Big Frank had said.

At eight-thirty the next morning a pair of stretch limos pulled out of *The Golden Nugget* parking lot and headed east on Sahara Avenue until they came to U.S. Highway 93. They turned north.

Cry Baby was in a funk. He hated to leave Vegas. It was home. He thought of it as his city. Or it would be, once his father was in a coffin.

In Vegas Cry Baby was somebody important, and he liked that. He liked that a lot.

Yuba City would be a whole different story. Hicksville, Cry Baby thought as his limo trailed the other off into the Nevada hinterlands. He'd never been there but he'd been through dozens of small towns like it on drug and gun and cigarrette runs to Aspen and L.A. and elsewhere.

No skyscrapers to blaze the night with neon, no casinos where the action never stopped.

Cry Baby was willing to bet that Yuba City rolled up its sidewalks at night. What in hell was his father thinking? he asked himself. Sending him to the middle of nowhere, all because of the Gambioso beef.

Cry Baby was tempted to pour himself a drink but his father had ordered him not to go on a bender, and once Cry Baby started, he found it hard to stop. He glared at the guy across from him, his resentment rising. Arty Johnson was half-soused. It was Johnson's radio station he was being sent to run. If the lame fuck hadn't taken a worthless marker, none of this would be happening. "Go easy on the sauce, hickweed. I need you able to walk when we get there."

Arty lowered the flask he'd been nursing since he woke up. He wanted to get plastered to deaden himself to the nightmare his life had become. His cherished radio station was no longer his. Ghouls in human guise had wrested it from him and would murder him without a qualm if he didn't obey their every whim. It couldn't get any worse. He held up his left hand and almost burst into tears. His poor finger. His poor station. Poor him. Wait until his wife found out. She'd throw a hissy fit to end all hissy fits.

Cry Baby folded his arms and sulked. He was a good sulker. He was almost as good at it as he was at holding a grudge. He decided then and there that the Gambiosos would pay for this insult. When he ran the Scarvetti organization, he'd settle their hash. He'd have the Gambioso bigwigs whacked, even if it meant war.

He stared at the others in the limo; Valentino, Switch and Dill. The latter was driving. If they were aware he was staring at them, they didn't show it, which was just as well for them, the mood he was in.

Val was thinking of the special instructions he'd been given. The night before, after Big Frank laid down the law to his son, Cry Baby had stalked off in a huff. He and Switch started to follow but Big Frank called him back.

"You heard what I said to Lou? I'm counting on you to keep an eye on him. Report to me immediately at the first sign of a problem."

"You still want to rely on me after I failed you?" Val

had asked in some surprise.

"How were you to know Lou would whack Scola?" Big Frank rejoined. "They were always at each other's throats. Nothing ever came of it until that last time. Between you and me, I think Scola was asking for trouble. Why else did he come to Vegas? And visit our casino, no less? Scola got his rocks off razzing people he hated and my son was at the top of his hate list. They were like a pair of pit bulls. They couldn't stand to be in the same room."

"Still, I let you down, Mr. Scarvetti. The second Lou opened the trunk and got out that crowbar, I should have called you."

"It would have been too late," Big Frank said. "What counts for me is that you tried to talk him out of it. You did all you could, Val. I have no complaints."

That was the highest compliment Big Frank ever paid anyone but Val wasn't satisfied. "I can't stand to let you down after all you've done for me."

"What's done is done. Now listen." Big Frank had lowered his voice. "I know the risk I'm taking. Lou doesn't realize the danger he's in. The Gambiosos are not going to stand for having one of their made men whacked. They've asked for a sit-down but Old Man Gambioso might try to have Lou hit before then. Until I meet with the other heads of the Families, I need Lou somewhere safe, somewhere the Gambiosos would never think to look for him.

"You think Lou will be safe in Yuba City?"

"Safer than here. If Old Man Gambioso does authorize a hit, you can bank on him dong his damnedest to find out where Lou got to. You and the rest of your crew must stay sharp. Fill them in but make it clear they're not to let Lou know that they're under special orders to babysit him. He'd fly off the handle and make matters worse."

Val had nodded. "Sure thing." He didn't like having so much responsibility but no one ever refused Big Frank.

"You're to stay with my son every minute of every day. Don't let him out of your sight, not even when he takes a leak. Any trouble, you get on the horn to me. You'll be put right through." Big Frank had risen and come around the desk. "I know this is rough on you, you being the youngest of your crew, and all. You're probably wondering why I rely on you so much and not one of the older guys."

Yes, Val had wondered that very thing.

"I'll give it to you straight. You're the youngest but you have the most street smarts. Truth is, I'd have you working for me here if I didn't need someone dependable to watch my son. The others all have flaws."

"Flaws?"

"Dill's brains are in a pickle jar. Switch has a quick mind to go with his quick hands but he's too much the good soldier to speak up even when Lou is out of line as he was with Scola. Pretty Boy can't tear his eyes off himself long enough to notice when something goes wrong. And the Wolfman is, well, the Wolfman."

"I'll do my best for you, Mr. Scarvetti."

Easier said than done, Val now mused as out of the corner of his eye he saw Cry Baby glare at everyone and everything in the limo. He almost wished he was in the front vehicle with Pretty Boy and the Wolfman. They were lucky. They got to ride with Eddy the Book and the lawyers.

A scraping noise intruded on his train of thought.

Switch had taken a whetstone from a pocket and was sharpening one of his switchblades.

He loved knives. Always had. When he was a kid he would sneak peaks at his father's hunting knife, a big bowie, and hold it to a lamp so the polished steel gleamed. He'd run his finger over the metal, so smooth and cool to the touch, admiring the craftsmanship.

The first knife Switch owned was a cheap penknife he stole from a corner market. With it he made his first kill, a toad some of the kids found in a vacant lot. He'd cut off it's hind legs and laughed as it flopped around, then cut off its front legs and the kids used it as a football. Later, just to see what was inside it, he'd opened its belly, spilling its guts over his sneakers.

From the penknife Switch had graduated to a dagger he'd bought at a pawn shop. It was double-edged, 420 stainless, sharp enough to slice a hair. He cut his fingers countless times running them over the razor edge. He also cut up a few punks. Nothing serious but he got a rep for being a bad dude with a blade.

Switch was seventeen when he broke his cherry. Not with girls, or by being busted by the Man. His cherry was his first switchblade, courtesy of a peddler who sold everything under the sun. A work of art, it had pearl handles and a blade that opened at the press of a button. Switch flicked it open so much, he nearly wore it out. When he wasn't practicing he would sit with the switchblade and fondle it. He gave it a name: Beauty. He still owned her. She was much too precious to risk damaging or losing so he kept her locked in a display case in his apartment.

Thinking of her, Switch ran the edge of one of his Italian imports across the whetstone. The rasp of metal on stone was music to his ears. Under his jacket he wore a special vest fitted with ten thin pockets, five on the right and five on the left. In each pocket was another switchblade.

He went to slide the one in his hand across the whetsone again and someone in the limo growled like an animal.

CHAPTER SEVEN

Cry Baby had taken the annoying scrape-scrape-scrape for as long as he could. "Do you have to do that now, fuckwad? Sharpen your toys on your own fucking time."

"Sorry, Mr. Scarvetti," Switch said, and quickly slid the switchblade into his vest.

Val could see the trip was going to be sheer hell unless he could get Cry Baby to lighten up. "Have you ever been to Yuba City, Mr. Scarvetti?" he asked. None of the crew were permitted to call him Lou. It had to be 'Mr. Scarvetti this' or 'Mr. Scarvetti' that.'

"No," Cry Baby snapped. "Who the hell would want to? What's to see? Fifteen yokels and a goat." He noticed that Arty Johnson had glued his mouth to the flask once more and kicked him in the shin. "Hickweed, I won't tell you again to put that away. And while you're at it, tell me about this stinking stickburg of yours."

Arty had been born and raised in Yuba City. He'd played on the Yuba High baseball team. He was a civic leader, a member of the chamber of commerce, and he disliked having his hometown put down by a know-nothing scumbag Mobster. "For your information, the population is almost fifty thousand. That's more than Winnemucca. More than Elko, too."

"Whip-de-fucking-do," Cry Baby said. "It wouldn't make a difference if it was a hundred thousand. They'd still be a hundred thousand hicks." Talking about it made Cry

Baby feel worse. To hell with it, he thought, and barked at Switch. "Fix me a drink. The usual."

Half a flask of vodka had lent Arty a smidgen of courage. "Quit calling us hicks," he said. "Yuba City is as modern as Las Vegas. We have a shopping mall, four theaters, three bowling alleys and---."

Cry Baby snorted. "Only hicks would think it was fun to roll a ball as big as an elephant's nut at a bunch of fake penguins."

"Even city folk like to bowl," Arty said defensively. "Just because you don't like something doesn't make it stupid. We have a skating rink. And video arcades. And Pizza Hut and all the fast food places, the big ones like McDonald's and Burger King. No Wendy's yet but we're working on it."

"Gag me with a spoon, dimbulb," Cry Baby said. "What about real food? Do you have any Italian restaurants? Or a place where I can get good steak, lobster or shrimp? Or those fish eggs I like, on toast?"

"Yuba City boasts an impressive number of four-star restaurants," Arty declared. "Our city council works hard to attract new businesses in order to make our city a decent environment for families to grow and prosper. We have our own TV station, a daily newspaper and three radio stations."

"Three? You mean I don't own the only one?"

"Goodness, no. Why would you think you did?"

"I don't know as I like that." Cry Baby raised his voice. "Dill, turn on the radio. I want to listen to my station."

Arty almost burst into tears. He'd slaved for decades to make his station a success. Having it stripped from him was like having his heart ripped from his chest. "You can't," he said.

"How's that again, dimbulb?"

"We aren't close enough to Yuba City yet," Arty explained. "We have to get over that mountain range up ahead and then we can pick it up."

"Fucking figures," Cry Baby groused. "What, I've got some kind of weak-ass station? That won't do." He sank back, feeling irritable.

Dill began to hum to himself and to tap on the steering wheel.

"Did I say you could do that, pickle dick?" Cry Baby asked. "Because if I didn't you sure as hell better stop before you tick me off."

Dill stopped.

Valentino gazed out the window at several horses running free in a field. He thought again about those in the front limo, and how lucky they were. At least they were all in a good mood.

Eddy the Book saw the horses but he hardly noticed them. He had succumbed to a rare fit of temper.

Eddy resented being sent to Yuba City. He resented having to nursemaid Cry Baby through the transfer. He resented Cry Baby, period. It had nothing to do with the younger Scarvetti's unbearable personality and everything to do with the fact Cry Baby was a bigot.

Eddy learned the truth by accident.

About a year ago he'd gone to see Big Frank about a discrepancy in the Accounts Receivables. The door to Big Frank's office was open and he heard voices. Not meaning to snoop, he'd listened to find out who Big Frank was talking to. It was Cry Baby.

To his surprise, they were talking about him.

"----why you keep that snot-nosed Eddy around, pops. If I was in charge, I'd boot him out the door and get one of our own to take care of the books. Know what I mean?"

"Don't ever let me hear you talk about Eddy like that again. He's been with me a long time, almost as long as the Iceman. I trust him, Lou."

"He's not even Italian, for crying out loud. He's as out of place in our Family as a darkie would be. Or a mick. When I take over, I'm going to surround myself with nothing but one hundred percent wops."

"Where do you get this from? You don't get it from me, that's for sure."

"Get what?"

"Your prejudice. You sound like a Nazi."

"How the fuck did skinheads get into it? All I'm saying is that I don't trust anyone who doesn't like pasta more than bagels. What did his kind ever do for us? For anyone, for that matter?"

"They gave the world two religions."

"They did? I thought---how do you say it?---Judaism? I thought that was the only one they have. Where they wear beanies and beat their heads against a wall and shit."

"They also gave the world Christianity."

"Get out of here. You're jerking my chain. They're not Christians. Hell, they don't even believe in Jesus."

"Jesus was born a Jew, Lou."

"No fucking way. He was Catholic, lke us. He started the Catholic Church. And the Pope is his main man here on earth. I didn't pay much attention the times you made me go to those hinky catechism classes when I was a kid but I remember that much."

"Leave."

"What?"

"Go do something. Get out of my sight before I forget myself and beat you with this ashtray."

"That's a fine way to talk to your son."

Big Frank had let out a sigh. "Sometimes you make me ashamed to be your father. Maybe I should have forced you into a seminary like your mother wanted. Maybe we would all be better off if you had become a priest."

A chair had scraped.

Eddy retreated to a stairwell before he was seen. He had watched Cry Baby swagger off, and from that moment on, Eddy hated him with every fiber of his being.

Eddy took pride in his heritage. He might not be the most Torah-true Jew who ever lived, but he believed. Because of his race, he'd suffered abuse and hatred. The last place he expected to encounter it was in the son of one of his closest friends.

Now, Eddy twisted and looked out the back window at the other limo. He half hoped a tire would blow out and Cry Baby would be thrown against a door and break his neck. As devoted as Eddy was to Big Frank, he couldn't take much more of the vile bastard Big Frank had spawned.

That morning, before they left Vegas, there was another incident.

Eddy and the attorneys were kept waiting for half an hour. They were supposed to leave Vegas at eight but could Cry Baby be on time? Of course not.

Eddy was mildly surprised when Cry Baby came over and took him aside. His skin had crawled when the younger Scarvetti draped an arm over his shoulders as if they were the best of buds.

"So, the two of us together, eh, Eddy? I know you don't

want to go and I don't blame you. My father is out of his fucking mind sending me to run a radio station. I don't know radio from spit. But we have to do as he says, don't we? And you have to do as I say, don't you?"

"Excuse me?"

"I'm in charge of the Yuba City operation. What I say, goes. I don't want you giving me any lip while you're there. None of those little digs of yours that really frost me. I'm putting you on notice, and putting you in your place. Get me?" Cry Baby had bestowed a spiteful smile.

Put me in my place, Eddy the Book fumed. He'd teach that son of a bitch. Somehow, someway, as sure as he lived and breathed, he would make Cry Baby pay.

CHAPTER EIGHT

For the next hour the two limos wound steadily on over rolling summits and along winding valleys. Dill and the Wolfman stuck to the speed limit out of habit. Big Frank was a stickler for avoiding cops. Speeding tickets were a no-no. He'd told all his soldiers the same thing: "Never give the law a reason to pull you over. Even if you're clean, they might set you up by planting something so they can haul you in for questioning."

Cry Baby hated that it was taking so long to get there. He forgot about listening to his new station until Dill began to hum again. "Shut up, pickle puss, and turn the radio on. I want to hear how good I sound."

"What station is it?" Dill asked.

Arty Johnson had dozed off. A poke in the ribs remedied that.

"We're over that range you were yapping about," Cry baby said. "How do we find my station?"

"It's on the FM side of the dial. The frequency is 101.7."

"Frequency?"

"What you would call the signal," Arty explained. 'FM is short for frequency modulation. It has a wider range of audio response than AM, or amplitude modulation. It's also more free from noise and---."

"Yeah, yeah. " Cry Baby hollered up to Dill. "FM. 101.7. Pipe it through in the back."

Quad speakers crackled to life with static. Dill went

down the dial and jazz filled the limo. Switch snapped his fingers to the beat, frowning when the jazz was replaced by the Beatles. On down the dial Dill went, past station after station. "It should be the next one, boss."

Cry Baby grinned like a kid about to be treated to an ice cream cone. Rubbing his hands in anticipation, he tilted his head toward a speaker.

More static crackled, then an electric guitar twanged and a voice crooned, "*I'm walkin' the streets over you, I can't help feelin' so blue, I was hopin', oh, so hopin', you'd be true, but now I'm walkin' the streets over you.*"

"What the hell was that?" Cry Baby said. "It sounded like hillbilly music. This is Nevada, not Tennessee." He shook his head. "That can't be my station. Go a little further, Dill."

"It's the right one," Arty said.

The song ended and a DJ with a pronounced drawl came on. "That was the great Ernest T. with his classic *Walkin' The Streets Over You* on Country 101, K-C-O-W. And this here is ol' Hoss reminding you of the K-COW jamboree the weekend after next."

Cry Baby sat back. "What the fuck did he just say? Did he just call my fucking station a fucking cow?"

"Those are the call letters," Arty said.

"The what?"

"K-C-O-W. They spell K-COW. Pretty catchy, eh?"

"You named it after a fucking cow? What kind of fucking moron are you? "

Arty sniffed indignantly. "Yuba City is in the heart of ranch and farm country, I'll have you know. Country music is tremendously popular. Granted, we're in second place in the ratings but that has nothing to do with our call letters.

When you think about it, you'll agree that K-COW is quite clever."

"Dipshit, I could think about it from now until fucking doomsday and I'd still think that naming a fucking radio station after a fucking cow is the stupidest fucking thing I've ever fucking heard." Cry Baby saw Valentino's mouth quirk upward. "Don't you dare laugh. None of you. It's my station now and I won't have anybody laughing at me."

"No, sir, Mr. Scarvetti."

Music blared, a pounding rhythm of drums and guitar. Another voice launched into another song. "*Lord, it's the same old beat we've been hearin' for years, fiddles and guitars and lots of tears. Where do we go from here? Get rid of the suits and those big motor cars. And Lord, get rid of the tears.*"

"Someone shoot me," Cry Baby said.

"That's Waylon, and Are You Sure We Have To Do It Thataway," Arty said. It was one of his favorites. "Surely you've heard of him? Good friends with Willie Nelson. They starred in some TV movies together. Waylon even sang the theme song for The Dukes of Hazard."

"The dukes of who?" Cry Baby recalled an oldie but goodie about the *Duke of Earl* but that was from back in the Stone Age. Something else had caught his attention. "What was that you said about being in second place?"

"Yuba City has three radio stations, remember? K-COW is always second in the ratings, just a few points behind K-W-I-N but ahead of K-D-L-R."

"KWIN? Now that I like." Cry Baby scratched his chin. "No one told me about this ratings stuff. I don't like being second at anything. How come my station isn't first? What kind of music does K-WIN play? More hickabilly?"

"Country, like us, yes," Arty confirmed. "We have

charts and stats that will break down the demographics for you. Essentially, what it boils down to is that they were on the air before we were and solidified a core audience that has stuck with them over the years. We have more listeners in the eighteen to thirty-four bracket but they have double what we do in the thirty-four to fifty demographic. So they squeak past us all the time."

"That won't do."

"Well, you're welcome to try to improve our numbers. But I've tried everything from hiring the best announcers that I could afford to throwing money away in promotions. KCOW still always comes in second."

"I'll set things right," Cry Baby vowed. "Wait and see."

Arty bit his lip to keep from saying something that might earn him another kick. Managing a radio station wasn't as easy as Scarvetti seemed to think. The man would learn. A station could have the best on-air talent and play the hottest hits and give away prizes galore but that was no guarantee it would come out on top in the ratings.

Cry Baby called out to Dill. "Go back up the dial until I tell you to stop. Do it slow."

The previous station came on and then the one before that, and more.

"Now go to fucking K-COW," Cry Baby directed. After Dill complied, he turned to Arty. "How come some of those other stations sound louder than mine? How come my station sounds so weak? Do we need stronger batteries or something?"

"It's not how loud a signal is but how clear it is that counts," Arty said. "Still, you have a point about signal strength. KCOW has a fifty thousand watt transmitter, so naturally those with a hundred thousand can come in stronger than we do."

"Why don't we have a hundred thousand dealie?"

"Because we're not licensed for one. The FCC won't allow it."

"The who?"

"The Federal Communications Commission. A branch of the federal government. They make the rules and regulations that control the use of the broadcast spectrum."

"The Feds, huh?" Cry Baby said in disgust. "I should have known they'd meddle in radio like they do everything else. But I don't like having a weak station any more than I like being second. Mark my words, Arty, my man. Before I'm done we'll have the most powerful station in Yuba City and be top station in those ratings, to boot."

Arty's impulse was to cackle but a bizarre thought struck him. What if this Mobster could do it? His dream would come true. But no, Arty mused. To pull it off, Scarvetti would have to accomplish a miracle.

To say nothing of bash a lot of heads.

CHAPTER NINE

They passed Hiko and were on a long stretch of highway flanked by emptiness. Cry Baby couldn't stop fidgeting. When they crested a hill he gazed down over a valley and spied a cluster of buildings. Of main interest to him was the gas station sign that reared high into the sky. Where there was a gas station there was a men's room and he had to take a leak in the worst way. "Dill, make a pit stop at that gas station. Val, get on the horn and let the other limo know."

In the first vehicle Pretty Boy was admiring himself in the rearview mirror. He kept twisting it to face him, much to the Wolfman's annoyance.

"I can't keep an eye on Mr. Scarvetti's car with you doing that."

"Relax, will you, Wolfy?" Pretty Boy said. "What's going to happen? Are you afraid aliens will swoop down and suck Cry Baby up into their flying saucer?"

The Wolfman wasn't amused. Pretty Boy was making fun of him because he liked to read supermarket tabloids. He was convinced *The Star* and *The Inquirer* were every bit as reliable as, say, *Time* or *Newsweek*. More so, since the tabloids reported things the big news organizations didn't cover. Like that family down in Mexico, the one where every newborn was completely covered with hair. It had something to do with genetics. But they didn't let their condition get them down. They went on with their lives, living as normally as they could.

Beeps from the car phone diverted Pretty Boy from the mirror. He answered the call.

The Wolfman took advantage and adjusted the mirror the way it should be, saying, "Now leave this alone."

Just then they passed a road sign that announced the hamlet of Elkhorn was a mile ahead.

"We're stopping there," Pretty Boy announced.

"What for?"

"Val didn't say. My money is on Cry Baby's bladder."

The Wolfman chuckled. Cry Baby couldn't drink a glass of water without having to run to the bathroom five minutes later. The Wolfman glanced at the side mirror and then at the rearview mirror---only to find, yet again, it was swiveled toward Pretty Boy. "Damn you."

"Now, now. I thought we were friends."

"We are. But you can be a pain in the ass."

Pretty Boy made sure his slicked hair was in place. His dark eyes twinkling, he admired his square jaw and perfect cheeks. He was aware that his infatuation with himself went way beyond what would be considered normal. He was also aware that he was the butt of as many jokes as Cry Baby's bladder. But he couldn't help himself. He honest to God couldn't.

It all started the day Pretty Boy's parents put a full-length mirror in his bedroom. Pretty Boy was ten. He'd spent every spare moment in front of it, posing, tilting his head this way and that, marveling at how gorgeous he was. Subsequent experience bore him out. In high school girls followed him home after school, called him unasked, even waited on his porch for him to come out in the morning.

Nowadays, when he went out on the town with the crew, women were all over him.

Pretty Boy tolerated their attention but he seldom acted on it. The truth was, women bored him. That, and few females could rival his own magnificence. He would rather look at himself than at them.

"Uh-oh," the Wolfman said.

Pretty Boy tore his gaze from the mirror. Near the gas station was a ramshackle building with a faded sign that proclaimed, *Ike's Wayside Tavern*. Parked in front were dozens of bikes, choppers lined up in row after row. Many had high-backed seats, extended forks, and enough chrome to chrome-plate a casino. "What?"

"Bikers."

"So? If we don't bother them, they won't bother us."

"I don't like bikers."

The Wolfman didn't tell him why. But once, when he was in his teens, his mother asked him to go to the pharmacy for her. He'd balked. It was the middle of the afternoon. Couldn't he wait until dark so no one could see him? So no one would point and stare?

His mother was adamant. "You're going and that's final. My nose is plugged. I wrote down what to get and here's the money."

The Wolfman had argued. He'd made her so mad, she booted his backside as she pushed him out the door.

The Wolfman had left by the back gate and stuck to alleys and side streets. The pharmacy was on the other side of a busy avenue. Intent on avoiding traffic, he'd darted across without noticing four bikers parked at the curb. Suddenly he was right on top of them.

They were members of a local gang, *Satan's Slayers.* One, in particular, the Wolfman would never forget. A biker with a belly as big as a beer keg and a scraggily beard that hung halfway to a studded leather belt.

The porker had snagged the Wolfman by the arm as he sought to scurry past. "Well, what do we have here?"

One of the others laughed. "God, look at him, Jack. He's the hairiest son of a bitch I've ever seen."

Jack had bent down, his breath reeking of onions. "What's your name, kid?"

"Vario. Richie Vario." The Wolfman tried to pull loose but the biker's grip was too strong. "Let go of me."

"Hold still or I'll tear your damn arm off." Jack had looked the Wolfman up and down. "Where in hell did you get all that hair?"

"I was born with it. What, you think I glued it on?"

Jack shook him, hard. "Don't be a smartass, boy." He'd poked the Wolfman's head and neck. "Jesus. You should be in a circus. Get people to pay to see you. All you'd have to do is sit on your ass and growl at them and you'd make more money than you'd know what to do with."

"I'm not no freak," the Wolfman angrily told him, and dug his fingernails into the biker's wrist. There was a jarring blow to his chin, and the world spun and jumped. When it settled again, the Wolfman was on his back with Jack standing over him.

"I should kick your ribs in. You scratched me, you ugly bastard."

Tears of frustration and hate had streamed down the Wolfman's cheeks, dampening his facial hair.

Jack nudged him with a boot. "Quit your blubbering. So what if you're a misfit? We all are, in one way or another."

"Maybe we should give him a shave," suggested a skinny Slayer.

"Nah," Jack said. "All the baby would do is bawl. Where's the fun in that?"

Their choppers roared off, and the Wolfman was alone. He'd slowly sat up, sniffling. "So what if I'm a misfit?" he'd shouted after them. "I'm still a person!."

Now, as he wheeled the limo toward the gas pumps, the Wolfman glanced at the bikes in front of the tavern and his mouth went dry. Another biker pulled in, a scarecrow in leather. A buxom blonde in a halter top was riding double. They got off and ambled inside.

The glass panel behind the front seat hissed down.

"Why are we stopping?" Eddy the Book asked. "Didn't you gas up before we left Vegas?"

"Sure did," the Wolfman said. "But Mr. Scarvetti wants to."

Eddy the Book cracked them all up by saying, "He must have swallowed some spit."

No sooner did the second limo stop than the object of their mirth dashed to the outside door to the men's room. Cry Baby cursed like crazy when the door wouldn't open. He smacked it and kicked it.

The Wolfman picked that moment to climb out and stretch his legs.

"Vario!" Cry Baby pointed at him. "The pisser is locked. Go in and get the fucking key."

"Right away, Mr. Scarvetti." The Wolfman hurried into the gas station.

It was a typical mom-and-pop operation, or in this

case, a grandmom-and-grandpop. Behind the counter were an elderly couple on stools, the woman knitting, the man watching a small TV with the volume off. Both raised their heads when the bell over the door tinkled.

The old man grunted and began to lower his head, then jerked it up. "Land sakes, I never saw the like."

"How may we help you, young man?" the grandmom asked, her smile positively saintly.

The Wolfman adored her on the spot. "Your restroom is locked."

"Sorry about that but we have no choice. There's too much vandalism these days. It's the kids. They don't respect property like my generation did." She deposited her knitting on the counter. "Now where did I put that key?"

The old man was mesmerized. "How about some razor blades, sonny?"

"No thanks."

"Are you sure? We have real ones. Twin-edge metal, not those plastic jobbies. I'll even throw in a razor, half price."

"I don't need one."

"Have you looked in a mirror lately?"

"Hush, pa," the grandmother said sternly. Folding her wrinkled hands in her lap, she gave the Wolfman another of those wonderful smiles. "I'm sorry, young man, but the key isn't here. I just remembered. One of those biker gentlemen asked for it a while ago and never brought it back. I imagine he's over at the tavern. Would you be a dear and fetch it for me?"

The Wolfman would rather pull out his wisdom teeth with pliers but he heard himself say, "Sure. No problem." Out the door he went, only to stop short as the reality sank in. Rock music blared from the tavern. A pair of hefty mongrels in leather were revving their machines.

"What the fuck is the holdup?" Cry Baby hollered. His hands over his crotch, he rocked up and down on the balls of his feet. "Why are you standing there like a fucking zombie? I need this fucking door unlocked."

"The key is at the tavern," the Wolfman said.

"What are you waiting for?" Cry Baby fumed. "Want me to carry you there? Go get it. I'm hurting, damn it."

The Wolfman knew better but he said, "Can't someone else do it, Mr. Scarvetti? Please?" He saw Pretty Boy admiring himself in the rearview mirror. "How about Sal?"

Cry Baby gurgled like a pipe about to burst. "How about I do to you what I did to Vic Scola?" He speared a finger at Ike's. "Get your fucking ass in there and get the fucking key or so help me God you'll spend the rest of your fucking days walking around with a fucking crowbar shoved so far up your fucking ass that you'll have to sneeze through your fucking ears."

Swallowing hard, the Wolfman walked toward the tavern, every step a needle driven into his chest. He was panic-struck. He stopped near the door, afraid to open it.

"Sometime this century, Vario!" Cry Baby yelled.

"Oh God," the Wolfman said.

CHAPTER TEN

A blast of cool air enveloped the Wolfman as the door was flung open from within. Several bikers emerged, giving him the once-over. Girding himself, the Wolfman entered..

The place was as big as a barn. Pool tables and pinball machines lined one side, a bar was on the other. In the middle were tables and a row of booths. Bikers were drinking, joking, smoking, fooling around.

The Wolfman was the only person in the whole joint wearing a suit. Feeling conspicuous in more ways than one, he hurried to the bar. No one was tending it, or so he thought until Moby Dick in leather heaved up from behind the counter holding two whiskey bottles. A grimy apron was tied around the bartender's stout waist. The man set the bottles down with a thump and reached for a glass, then saw the Wolfman.

"What the hell? Where did you come from?"

"Next door. The old lady sent me for the key."

"Key? What key?"

"To their restroom," the Wolfman said. "She says that someone in here used it and never brought it back."

"Is that so?" Moby Dick gestured at the bikers. "Make the rounds. It shouldn't take you more than a few minutes to find out who has it."

Knowing Cry Baby as he did, the Wolfman didn't have a few minutes. "I'd be grateful if you could help me out. It's sort of an emergency."

"How grateful?"

"Ten dollars worth," the Wolfman said. That seemed reasonable, especially since the ten would come out of his pocket.

Moby Dick stuck a thick finger in his ear and wriggled it. "My hearing must be going. I could have sworn you said you needed it right away."

The Wolfman resented being taken advantage of but he fished out his wallet. "Will twenty do?"

Snatching the bill, the bartender chortled. "I would have settled for the ten if that was all you'd fork over." Bracing both hands on the bar, he exhibited surprising agility by swinging his legs up, and standing. Another song had just kicked in on the jukebox, Cream and *Sunshine Of Your Love*. "Kill the music," he shouted.

A biker whose arms were tattooed from his shoulders to his wrists reached behind the jukebox and yanked on the cord. The music promptly died.

All eyes swung to Moby Dick. And to the Wolfman. Few were friendly. The Wolfman plastered a grin on his puss and prayed the bikers had betters things to do than beat the snot out of him.

"What's up, Ike?" somebody shouted.

"And what's with the freaky dude with all the hair?" another hollered. "Is a sideshow passing through?"

Ike grinned. "We've got an emergency. Seems someone has to take a leak over to Ma's but they can't because one of you took the key and didn't give it back. So fork it over before I have a puddle on my floor."

Hoots and howls greeted the request.

The Wolfman was going to say that he wasn't the one who needed to use the restroom but he decided why bother.

Expectantly, he scanned the room but no one stepped forward.

"Come on, give this dude a break," Ike said. "Who has it?"

"I do."

The Wolfman turned.

Between the tables and the pinball machines stood five bikers. A pipsqueak with a shock of red hair and a thin red mustache held a key attached to a large wire ring.

The Wolfman's gut churned. He had a feeling it was going to be the *Satan's Slayers* all over again.

"Looking for this, furface?" the pipsqueak taunted. "How much is it worth to you?"

Ike came to the Wolfman's defense. "Come on, Killer. Cut the guy some slack. All he wants is to go to the bathroom. Why hassle him?"

"Shut up, Ike," the pipsqueak snarled, and to the Wolfman's surprise, Ike did. Apparently the handle 'Killer' was more than a nickname.

"All I want is the key.," the Wolfman said.

Smirking, Killer held it over his head. "Come and get it if you think you're man enough."

"I don't want any trouble."

Killer cackled like someone zoned on the hard stuff. "He doesn't want any trouble," he mimicked in a mincing tone. "Well, you've got trouble, hairball." He cocked his head. "Do you know who you remind me of?"

"No."

"The kid on that old TV show, the one with the monsters. Where Frankenstein is the dad and they have a dragon under the stairs. I see it on the tube now and then. What's it called?"

"The Addams Family," piped up a woman whose shorts were trying to crawl up her plump behind.

Another biker shook his head. "No. Addams Family was the one with the hand in the box."

"Yeah, Cousin It," said another. "That hairy sucker who shed all over the place."

Killer scowled. "That's not the show I'm thinking of. It was another one with a hairy sucker, where they drove a bitchin' coffin."

"Wasn't that The Monkees?"

The Wolfman had taken all he could. "The show was The Munsters. Fred Gwynne starred as the father, Herman, the Frankenstein character. Yvonne De Carlo played his wife, Lily. Al Lewis was Grandpa, a vampire. Butch Patrick played Eddy, the werewolf. He had a werewolf doll he called 'Woof Woof.'" It was his favorite show. He had the entire run on DVD and watched them regularly.

"Son of a bitch," Killer said. "I bet you're a wizard at Trivia Scruples."

"It's called Trivial Pursuit," the Wolfman said, and continued with his show of shows. "The Munsters lived at 1313 Mockingbird Lane in Mockingbird Heights. There car was a converted hearse, not a coffin, called the 'Munster Koach.' Their pet dragon was named 'Spot.'"

Killer's thin mustache twitched. "If there's one thing I hate, it's a know-it-all. Almost as much as I hate muties." He motioned and he and his companions closed in.

All of the Wolfman's childhood fears resurfaced in a tidal wave. Then he realized what the pipsqueak had said. "What did you just call me?"

"A mutant. You know, like in those comic books and movies where there's a guy covered in blue fur and the runt with claws that pop out of his hands."

This was a first. All the names the Wolfman had been called over the years, all the ridicule he'd endured, and no one had ever accused him of being a mutant. The stupidity of it snuffed his fear like wind snuffing a candle. "Give me the key and I'll forget how dumb you are."

"Will you, now?" Killer said. "What if I don't want you to forget? What if I want to pound your hairy head into the floor for the fun of it? What then?"

"Then I hope you have dental insurance," the Wolfman said, and taking a long stride, he punched the pipsqueak in the mouth. It sent Killer staggering. His triumph was fleeting. The other four were on him before he could set himself. He landed a couple of solid blows but there were too many. He was battered back against the bar. Dimly, he heard Ike bellowing for them to stop.

Rock-hard fists rained. Tucking his chin to his chest, the Wolfman protected his head with his arms. It left his body open but there was nothing he could do. He figured on being beaten senseless. Then his arms were seized and he was held helpless.

"You're in for it now, mutie." Killer was bleeding from a pulped lower lip. He bent and swooped his hand to his right boot and unfolded holding a bone-handled skinning knife. "Any last words?"

"Bite me," the Wolfman said.

"I'm going to enjoy this."

Bright metal flashed but it wasn't Killer's weapon. A slender blade slashed across Killer's wrist, drawing blood. Killer screamed and tried to back away. Again the metal streaked, slicing Killer's cheek.

Switch was there.

Killer tried to defend himself but he was no match for the blond wiseguy. In a blur, Switch cut Killer twice and Killer went down, shrieking in terror.

The bikers holding the Wolfman had problems of their own.

Pretty Boy and Dill waded in. A biker clipped Dill a good one but Dill shrugged it off and unleashed a haymaker that started near the floor and crumpled the biker like a piece of paper.

Pretty Boy was grinning. He always grinned in a fight. He wasn't as strong as Dill or as skilled with a knife as Switch or as down and dirty a street brawler as Val, but he had moves that had to be seen to be believed. Pure razzle-dazzle, he tore into a biker with a flurry of punches and kicks that left the man on his knees, gurgling and spitting blood. He always took opponents down swiftly so they wouldn't have a chance to hurt his face.

Valentino was up against a biker twice his size. The man's groin, the eyes, the throat were his targets.

More bikers rose and rushed to aid their friends. The outcome was inevitable. There were six bikers for every wiseguy. Ike, the owner, was bawling for everyone to calm the hell down and chill the hell out but blood was in the air as well as on the floor.

Switch swung toward the onrushing leatherstorm, a bloody switchblade in each hand. "Come and get some."

The bikers produced knives of their own. Chains were unwound. Chairs were raised.

That was when the tavern resounded to the thunder of two shots. Wiseguys and bikers alike turned toward the entrance.

Cry Baby stood just inside. He held a pair of nickel-plated Astra Model A-80's. Hunched over, his legs bent inward, he shambled forward like *The Creature From The Black Lagoon*. He even looked a shade of green around the gills. "What the hell is wrong with you, blowhole?" he demanded, jabbing a pistol at the Wolfman. "I send you for a key and you start a fucking riot?" His hands shook, his face twitched. "It doesn't matter if you're the son of the best friend of some bimbo my dad knew back in Chi Town. Screw up like this again and I'll have your balls nailed to a wall."

A biker moved, and just like that, Cry Baby sent a slug into the floor between his legs. "Mess with me. Someone *please* mess with me." Stopping, he glared at the motley assemblage. "Listen up. I want the fucking key to the pisser next door. I want the fucking key now. I want the fucking key before I see how many lame fucks I can fucking shoot before I fucking run out of fucking ammo." Livid, he pointed his pistols. "Who the fuck has it?"

The Wolfman gestured at Killer, who was on his back on the floor, quaking and clutching his bloody leg. "He does. But he wouldn't give it to me."

"Is that so?" Grimacing, Cry Baby took a staggering step and trained an Astra on Killer. "Hand it over, buttwipe. I won't tell you twice."

"I don't have it!" Killer screeched. "I dropped it. I don't know where it got to."

Cry Baby scanned the floor and then glanced down at himself. "Damn it. These are two hundred dollar pants. Vario, front and center."

The Wolfman scampered over. "Sir?"

"Unzip me."

"Sir?"

"Are you hard of fucking hearing? Unzip me while I cover your dancing partners. It's too late for the key."

The Wolfman could feel his skin burn under his hair as he did as Cry Baby wanted. He'd never been so humiliated in his life, and that took some doing.

"Now take my pecker out and hold it so I can piss."

A biker babe tittered.

"I'm sorry, Mr. Scarvetti," the Wolfman said. "With all due respect, I wouldn't do that even for your father."

"Weinie." Cry Baby motioned at Dill. "Picklepuss, get your big ass over here and you do it."

"Not me, boss. I draw the line at holding peckers."

"Son of a bitch. I have to do everything myself." Cry Baby angrily shoved an Astra at the Wolfman. "Cover these lameoids while I tend to business." Frantically unzipping, he freed his manhood and arced a yellow stream at the bikers, who scrambled madly to avoid being splashed. "Ahhhh," Cry Baby said in sheer bliss. He peed and peed.

"I waxed that floor last night," Ike grumbled.

Cry Baby happily zipped up. "There. Now do you fucking morons suppose we can get this fucking show on the road?" He spun and tramped to the door, and looked back. "As for you leather fucks, any word of this leaks to the fucking law and this fucking dump will be a fucking crater by the end of the fucking week."

No one tried to stop the wiseguys as they walked out. The Wolfman was last, covering their backs. As the door swung shut he overheard two bikers.

"Who were those dudes?"

"Beats me. That pisser was stone cold psycho."

CHAPTER ELEVEN

"Watch over my son like you're his guardian angel," were Big Frank's parting words to Valentino the night before Cry Baby's crew left Las Vegas for Yuba City.

Val intended to do the elder Scarvetti proud. No one could question his loyalty. The way Val saw it, he was in Big Frank's debt, a debt he could never repay. Hadn't Big Frank plucked him off the streets and made him a wiseguy? Hundreds of connected guys would give anything to be in his shoes. But Big Frank picked him, a nobody, a punk kid with no prospects, for the honor of honors.

Five years ago, it was.

Big Frank was on one of his frequent trips to the Windy City. He liked to visit the old neighborhood to keep in touch with his roots. He'd spend time with relatives, visit old haunts, play cards with guys he grew up with.

Whenever word spread that Big Frank was back, people in need flocked to see him. No problem was too big or too small. Big Frank always had a solution and he never asked anything in return. Not right away, anyway. Those in his debt didn't mind. He was their protector, their friend, their godfather.

Franco Scarvetti was one of the last of the Old School Dons, and the people in his community---the Italian community---loved him. He was one of them. He talked like them, acted like them. When they went to see him, they'd didn't go on bended knee. He would have none of that. He greeted them as equals and bid them call him Big Frank.

Five years ago Val was living like a stray mongrel on the street. He had no parents, no siblings, no home. His father had bailed on his mother when he was seven and his mother took refuge in the bottle and never came out. When he was fifteen her liver decided, 'Why bother'? Rather than become a ward of the state, Val lived in an abandoned tenement on the seediest block in the worst part of the city. By day he slept. At night he prowled, mingling with the addicts and the pushers, the pimps and the badasses who claimed the streets as their own from dusk until dawn.

At first Val was scared to death. Afraid someone would stick a blade in his ribs or split his head while he slept. A few close calls taught him that in order to survive he must observe and learn, and learn fast. He must get each lesson right the first time because there might not be a second chance.

His career choices weren't the kind open to white bread college grads.

Val developed a fondness for the ladies and toyed with the idea of becoming a pimp. But to quote Slick Leroy, the flesh peddler he most admired: 'Bitch, bitch, bitch. That's all them bitches do. Want to go crazy? Listen to those bitches bitch all day. They wag their tongues more than they wag their asses. Always wantin' more bread, more threads, more this, more that. Bitches ain't never satisfied. Give a bitch fifty dollars at eight, she'll be back at nine sayin' she needs fifty more. And talk about lazy. If it was up to them, they'd pull one trick a night. You have to slap them bitches around at least once a week just to keep them in line. Then there's the tears. God, don't get me started on the tears. When they get to missin' their mommas or thinkin' what they're doin' is wrong 'cause they're breakin' the Commandments on the Mount or some shit, you get tears and more tears. Spare me from bitches who think. If they'd let their snatches do their thinkin', they'd be a lot better off."

Val decided pimping wasn't for him.

Being a pusher held no appeal, either. Not when Val saw what drugs did, up close and personal. Hardly a month went by that someone Val knew didn't O.D. The worst was a kid he'd befriended, an eight-year old who showed up after Val had been living in the tenement about half a year. The kid was a nobody, just like him. Val took him under his wing, or tried to. Half the time the kid wouldn't listen. Thought he knew it all and had to do things his way. A pusher sucked the kid in and got him hooked on crack. From there it was a hop, skip and a snort to the morgue

Val was at the kid's side at the end. He held the kid's hand as the kid bawled and screamed and puked and begged God Almighty for the pain to end. It did, but not the way the kid wanted. Val would never forget that pasty, sweaty face, twisted in torment, the teeth bared, foam flecking his mouth as if the kid had rabies.

It was along about then that Val decided he hated yuppies. The pampered brats from the suburbs in their shiny cars and SUV's who cruised into the city on Friday nights and the weekends to score. The ones who had it all. Halfway decent parents, a good home, nice clothes. Who never had to worry where their next meal came from. Whose toughest challenge each day was to beat their favorite video game.

To the yuppies, drugs were recreation, drugs were fun.

They were jerkoffs. They had everything Val didn't, everything he craved, but they were too stupid to realize how good they had it. It got so, he despised the sight of them and their fancy wheels.

One night Val saw a freckle-faced yuppie go into a crack house. On an impulse he broke into the guy's sports car and helped himself to a case of CD's and a wallet the idiot had shoved under the front seat. The wallet contained two hundred and sixty-four dollars.

Val had found his calling. He'd teach the spoiled brats a lesson by ripping them off. He became a pro at jimmying locks, at stripping stereos from consoles, at finding secret stashes. A loose network of shady pawnshop owners and assorted customers kept him in the green. It didn't qualify him for *Lifestyles Of The Rich And Famous* but he got by.

One evening, late, Val came strolling around a corner and stumbled on a cash cow ripe for milking. It was a stretch limo that seemed to take up half the block. His brain boggled at the riches that must be inside. He cased it carefully. It was parked in front of a barbershop with a CLOSED sign in the window. No lights were on inside. No one was around.

Val took the plunge. Out came his tools. The lock was easy. With a pencil flashlight between his teeth, he was studying the expensive setup when the door opened and rough hands seized him. Val fought but there were four men in dark suits, hard men with hard fists they knew how to use. He was on his hands and knees on the sidewalk, spitting blood, when a voice rang out.

"Enough."

The men in the suits stepped back. Gentler hands

helped Val to stand and leaned him against the limo. He looked up at his benefactor, whose head was framed by a bright halo from an outside light that had come on above the barber shop.

Franco Scarvetti had given Val the once-over. "It's just a kid."

"He broke into the limo, boss," one of the men said. "He would have cleaned it out if Bruno hadn't spotted him."

"You've got balls, kid," another said. "No brains but lots of balls."

"I'm Big Frank," Franco Scarvetti introduced himself. He'd cupped Val's chin and turned his head from side to side. "You're Italian."

"Yes, sir," Val had mumbled through mashed lips.

"Let me guess. You're living on the street. No family. No one and no place to call your own."

They weren't questions. They were statements of fact. Val had stared up at the big man with the kindly eyes, confused, wondering what the guy was going to do.

"We're all Italians here," Big Frank said, motioning. "All paisans. All of the same blood. That makes us family. Can you see that?" Big Frank had straightened. "What's your name?"

"Michael Corcione."

"A Sicilian name. A name of distinction. A name to be proud of." Big Frank took a white silk handkerchief from an inner pocket and wiped blood from Val's mouth and chin. "Do you honor your blood by what you do? Is this how you show respect for your forefathers? By living as a petty thief?"

"I don't know what else---," Val had started to say, an

odd constriction in his throat.

"Look at me, boy," Big Frank commanded. "How would you like to come work for me? I can use someone like you. Someone who's street smart, someone who knows the score. It's your decision. Maybe the most important of your life. You can go on living like an animal or you can live like a man and hold your head high. Think it over. If you're interested, be here tomorrow night at eight."

Only an idiot would have refused.

Now, as Val walked with Cry Baby and the others up the walk to the radio station, he remembered that night, and was grateful for the great trust Big Frank had placed iin him. He vowed to prove worthy of the man who had saved him from the gutter.

CHAPTER TWELVE

Arty Johnson pointed at the bright red letters that spelled KCOW. "This used to be the Regency Theater before I bought it and had it converted. It cost a lot but it was worth every penny. Talk about a prime location. We're right in the heart of Yuba City. Everyone who works downtown, everyone who comes to shop or see a movie at the Bijou, sees our call letters.

"Be still my beating heart," Cry Baby said. He was bored to tears. The past half hour, the guy had jabbered up a storm, acting as if they were bosom buds. It made him suspicious.

As for the building, Cry Baby knew a dump when he saw one. It was all brick and stone, with the eye appeal of a shoe box. None of the glass and plastic Cry Baby liked, and only one story high. He was about to say, 'Big fucking deal', when he remembered what his father said to him the last time they talked.

"You're a businessman now, Lou. Act the part. Show some class. Clean up that garbage mouth of yours. Forget those silly movies and that TV show. Hollywood is make-believe. This is real life, and in real life people don't go around saying fuck every time they open their mouth. Talk filth and people think you're filth." His father had put a hand on his shoulder. "Do it for me, Lou. I've never asked much but I'm asking this."

Cry Baby stopped and surveyed downtown Yuba City.

Sidewalks so clean you could eat off them. No litter, no bums, no homeless. Sure, it was hick city, a throwback to the days of *Leave It To Beaver*, but it was his city now. Those pedestrians in their spiffy suits and pretty dresses were his people. They had to learn to accept that, to look up to him with respect as his father was looked up to and respected.

If cleaning up his act would help, so be it. He'd give it a try.

Using the f-bomb came so naturally, though, that stopping wouldn't be easy. Cry Baby realized he couldn't stop cold turkey. Not with his temper. He was bound to slip up. Maybe what he needed to do was replace the f-bomb with something else. But what? he wondered. It needed to be something easy to remember.

"Say, Mr. Johnson," Dill unexpectedly spoke up. "Where's the nearest store? I'm out of frigging pickles."

Frigging. Cry Baby smiled. It was perfect. He tried it on for size with, "Forget the frigging pickles, you frigging pickles-for-brains. Buy the frigging things on your own frigging time."

"Sure, boss," Dill said. "I was only asking."

Cry Baby cackled, and his crew all stared. "No frigging problem,." He turned to Arty Johnson. "As for you, you frigging lush, let's have the grand tour. This frigging dump better be all you frigging claim it is."

Switch glanced at Val and silently mouthed the word, 'Frigging'?'

Val shrugged to show he had no idea what had gotten into Cry Baby. Moving ahead, he held the door open. Eddy the Book and the lawyers were the last to enter, and he followed.

Cry Baby stopped in the reception area. He hadn't

seen such a lousy decorating job since that time he visited *The Bunny Ranch*. The walls there had been hot pink, the ceiling citrus orange, the carpet a bright shade of purple. It was supposed to be cheery and make the johns feel at ease but all it made him want to do was puke.

KCOW wasn't much better. The walls were a putrid brown. Wood, too, not plastic, like Cry Baby liked. On the right wall someone had painted a smiling cowboy on a white horse. On the left wall was a rodeo scene, with a rider astride a snorting bull. Cry Baby thought that was bad enough. Then he looked up.

Staring down at him was a huge cow wearing a Stetson and framed by the station's call letters.

"Isn't the artwork magnificent?" Arty Johnson crowed. "I hired a local artist, Susie Rainwater, to do it before she became famous. She's Paiute, you know."

"There's a frigging cow on the frigging ceiling," Cry Baby said.

"Visitors always comment on what a fine work of art it is," Arty enthusiastically gushed.

"It has to go."

"Are you serious? Everyone loves Susie Rainwater's work. Why, the Yuba City Tribune did a write-up on it. They plastered the K-COW cow over a two-page spread in their Sunday supplement. There's nothing in the world like free publicity, I always say."

"Find me someone to paint over this crap," Cry Baby instructed, "and we'll have the newspaper do a write-up on that, too."

"You have a lot to learn about running a business," Arty said, miffed.

"I know frigging stupid when I see it." Cry Baby

bobbed his chin at the giant cow. "That's as frigging stupid as it gets." He smoothed his tie. "Now show me to my office. I just hope to God you don't have a stuffed horse's ass over the desk."

Val didn't move on when the others did. His gaze was glued to the receptionist, who stared at him in sweet innocence. She was jaw-droping gorgeous.

Hair the color of spun gold framed a face fit for an angel. She had sparkling blue eyes, full red lips, and a complexion as flawless as a model's. When she smiled, her teeth gleamed like in one of those toothpaste commercials. Her voice was positively musical. "Hello there. Can I get you something?"

Val drank in the sight of her. There was plenty she could do for him, involving the two of them in their birthday suits. A witty retort was on the tip of his tongue, a pickup line he'd used a zillion times on showgirls, but something stopped him. He couldn't bring himself to say it. For the first time in his life, he was tongue-tied.

"Are you all right?" she asked. "You look a little peaked. Would you care for a glass of water?"

Val coughed. "No," he said, his voice strangely strained. "I just---that is---I don't---." He stopped. He was making a fool of himself.

The angel continued to smile. "Let me know if you do. I'm Misty, by the way. Who might you be?"

Val went to answer, and couldn't. His mind had gone blank, like a slate wiped clean. He couldn't remember his own name. It was too stupid for words. Thankfully, Switch came to his rescue by popping out of a doorway.

"Val, get in here. Mr. Scarvetti wants all of us in on

this."

"Is that your name?" the young woman said. "Val?"

"My nickname," Val said.

"I hope we get to talk again sometime. Nice meeting you."

"Nice. You," Val stammered, and hurried past. His skin was hot and his ears burned. And why? Over a woman. No, not even that, over a girl. An admittedly hot girl in a flowery cotton dress but still a girl. What in hell was happening to him? he wondered as he walked into the office.

"Nice to see you could make it, Corcione," Cry Baby said sarcastically. He was seated behind an oak desk. "What, you couldn't tear your frigging eyes off all that great frigging artwork?"

Val prudently kept quiet.

"Listen up, dimbulbs," Cry Baby barked. "Here's how we're going to play this. Johnson, I want you to find a room my crew can use, then make it clear to your people that no one is to bother them for any frigging reason at any frigging time. Which reminds me. Spread the word that all the employees are to show up for a meeting in an hour. I mean all of them. Whoever doesn't show is out on their can. At the meeting you'll introduce me as the new owner and I'll lay down the rules." Cry Baby saw Arty Johnson open and close his mouth. "You have something to say, hickstick?"

"I might not be able to round up everyone," Arty said.

"Why the hell not?"

"An announcer has to be on-air at all times. The sales staff are usually pounding the pavement at this time of day. And there's no telling where my chief engineer is. He comes and goes pretty much as he pleases."

"Not any more. All that changes as of now. No one goes anywhere or does anything without my say so." Cry Baby propped his shoes on the desk. "Who was that bimbo out front? The one who looks like she just stepped off the farm?"

"Misty Lane. Don't let her looks fool you," Arty said. "She's extremely competent. She handles the phones, greets visitors, types letters. She knows shorthand, she can write copy. Hell, she can even fill in on the board in emergencies. She's our Jane of all trades."

"Isn't that frigging cute?" Cry Baby snickered. "From now on she's to keep track of where everyone is. Have her whip up a sign-out sheet. And I want a list of all the people who work for me, their names and their addresses. Plus, I want to talk to this engineer you mentioned and set him straight about a few things."

Arty stifled a grin. No one set Howard Branigan straight on anything. "I should warn you. Engineers can be very temperamental and we can't afford to lose him. If you want my advice, you'll treat Howard with kid gloves."

"When I want your frigging advice, I'll frigging ask for it. But don't worry. I know how to persuade people to do what I want." A rumble from Dill's gut brought Cry Baby's head up. "That reminds me. I spotted a burger joint down the street. Val, since you're nearest to the door, I elect you to go get burgers, fries and shakes for the whole crew."

"Will do."

"Take the bimbo at the front desk to help carry the stuff. If she gives you any lip, tell her she can go hump herself and I'll hire someone to take her place."

Val wanted nothing more than to talk to Misty Lane

again. So long as he could get his tongue to work.

"Are you hard of hearing, dog dip?" Cry Baby asked. "Why are you still standing there? Go get the frigging food, already. Or is there a problem?"

Val thought of Misty, of her lustrous hair and those luscious lips. "No problem at all," he said.

CHAPTER THIRTEEN

Misty Lane was on the phone, a finger in her other ear so she could hear over the music coming from a speaker high on the wall. She didn't see Val walk up to the desk. He stood so close, he could caress her hair if he wanted. His mouth went dry, just like before. He figured he must be coming down with something. What other explanation was there? He didn't know this girl. She was nothing to him.

Misty hung up, swiveled, and gave a start, her hand flying to her throat. "Goodness!" You scared the living daylights out of me."

Get a grip, Val scolded himself, and offered his hand. "Sorry. My real name is Michael Corcione, by the way."

"How do you do. Again."

Her grip was soft but firm, her palm pleasantly warm, the feel of her skin on his like the feel of fine silk. Was it Val's imagination or did she let her fingers linger longer than was called for?

"Which do you prefer?"

"Sorry?"

"Val or Michael or Mike?"

"I'm used to Val," Valentino said, and coughed. "I need to get some food. The boss says you're to tag along."

"I am?"

"I'm honored to have your company," Val said, and bowed like Errol Flynn in one of those old movies, feeling stupid but doing it anyway.

"That Mr. Johnson," Misty said. "He always has me running errands. I try to tell him I can't get my work done when he has me scurrying all over the place but he never listens." She retrieved her purse from under the desk. "Where are we going?"

"Just down the street." Val smiled and pulled out her chair for her. "After you."

"My, aren't you the gallant gentleman," Misty teased. "I can't remember the last time a man did that for me."

"Have a lot of guys after you, do you?" Val bantered, and was troubled that the thought bothered him. What the hell was going on?

Misty laughed merrily. "Hardly, Mr. Corcione. Oh, I had dates in high school. Nothing serious, though. At the moment I'm seeing Jesse Stillwell. Maybe you know him? His family owns the ranch out on 62."

"I'm new to Yuba City," Val enlightened her, and made a mental note to meet Mr. Stillwell at the earliest opportunity. They made for the entrance, walking so close their arms brushed. She seemed not to notice. "You're the first person I've met from around here besides Arty."

"Really? Well, on behalf of the good people of Yuba City, allow me to welcome you. You'll love it here. Yuba City is the friendliest place in the whole U.S. of A. People go out of their way to be neighborly."

Val held the door for her. As she went by, he inhaled a fragrance that brought to mind a flower shop. She was a walking bouquet.

"Is something wrong, Mr. Corcione? You have that strange look again."

"I'm fine." Val smiled. "And call me Val, remember? Mr.

Corcione is too formal. Besides, I'm not much older than you."

Misty walked with the limber grace of a country girl, her dress clinging to her long legs. The breeze made golden streamers of her hair.

Val's own legs, strangely, didn't want to work as they should. He shuffled along as if feet were all toes, unable to take his eyes off her. He knew he should keep his mind on business, on Cry Baby and his responsibility to Big Frank. But Misty Lane mesmerized him. She was so different, so unlike the Vegas hoofers and other women he usually went out with. So unlike any woman he'd ever met. "How long have you been seeing this Stillwell?" He tried to sound casual but he didn't entirely succeed, earning an intent scrutiny from those piercing baby-blues of hers.

"About a year now. Why do you ask?"

"Just curious." In no hurry to part company, Val slowed so it would take them longer to reach the burger joint. "A year, huh? The two of you must be tight as can be."

"What do you mean by tight?"

"You know. An item. Humping heavy."

Misty Lane stopped. "Humping?"

Val couldn't believe she'd hadn't heard the expression. "Going at it like minxes." When she still didn't seem to get what he was saying, he elaborated. "Come on. What guys and gals do all the time. You and him, doing the bedsheet tango." He pumped his hips to illustrate.

"I don't know as I like you very much," Misty said.

"What? Why? What did I do?"

"My personal life is none of your business. But for your information, I'll have you know that Jesse and I have never---," Misty blushed a deep red, "---humped. Never done the bedsheet tango, as you put it. I'd never allow him to touch me there, and it's rude of you to even bring the subject up."

Val was trying to absorb what she'd just told him. It had to be a put-on. "Are you going to stand there and tell me that you've been dating this guy for a year and the two of you have never made love?"

Misty averted her gaze. "I don't know how it is where you come from but around here men don't ask ladies questions like that. Since you have asked, I'll tell you that no, we haven't ever made love."

"You're kidding."

"I'm saving myself for my wedding bed," Misty informed him. "I know it's not the thing to do in this day and age but I live as I see fit and not as everyone else does."

"You've never----?"

"Never, ever. Now may we please talk about something else or not talk at all?" Angry, Misty walked on, her heels clicking sharply.

The full implication hit Val with the impact of a wrecking ball. She'd never slept with a man. Her lush body was as pure as----what was that saying? Oh, yeah. As pure as the driven snow. Whatever the hell snow had to do with anything.

Another thought jarred him.

If she'd never had sex, that made her a virgin.

"God in heaven," Val blurted.

"Pardon me?" Misty said over her shoulder.

"Nothing," Val replied. But he sensed, deep down, that it was everything.

CHAPTER FOURTEEN

The entire staff showed up for the meeting due to Misty Lane's efforts. She was able to track everyone down. Puzzled and curious, they gathered in the KCOW break room.

Arty moved to the front to get their attention. Truth to tell, he was so excited, he could hardly stand still. The more he talked to Lou Scarvetti, the more convinced he became that the Mobster might actually pull it off, might make KCOW number one in the ratings for the first time ever.

As much as Arty hated what had happened in Vegas, as much as he resented having the station taken from him, he wanted to be numero uno more than anything. It had been his dream since he could remember. Just once he'd like to be able to walk up to Cleve Richards, the snooty owner of KWIN, shove the Blue Book under Cleve's haughty snoot, and crow like a rooster. Just once.

Arty surveyed the break room, studying his people. Correction, his former people. They were Scarvetti's staff now.

At a table on the right sat the announcers in their own little clique. Hoss was there, their morning man, a roly-poly bear with a bushy beard he was forever stroking. Next to him sat Smoky Williams, their night man. Smoky always wore jeans, a Roy Rogers shirt, and a flat-crowned black hat, the kind gamblers and gunfighters used to wear in the Old West. Susie Q was at the end of the table. She worked the afternoon drive. No one listening to her soft voice would guess she weighed almost as much as Hoss. She was shaped like a donut, which was fitting since she ate them for breakfast, lunch and dinner. The last announcer was Duke Banner. His passion was John Wayne. He owned every movie Wayne ever made and owned enough John Wayne memorabilia to fill a warehouse. He even dressed like the Duke. The only thing was, where the real Duke had been an imposing man with a forceful presence, Duke Banner was four-feet-seven inches in his high-heeled cowboy boots, and was about as imposing as a cricket. He had a voice as deep as the Grand Canyon, though. Half their female listeners were in love with it.

At a table on the left sat the station Program Director, Larry Todd. As PD, Larry was in charge of the work schedules, the music they played, and a hundred and one things Arty would otherwise have to do.

The two members of the sales staff were at another table. Billy Holliday and Sam Dowd had been at KCOW for ten months and six months, respectively. Billy had sold used cars after high school, then worked a short stint at KDLR before Arty hired him. Dowd was an older guy, grey at the temples. He'd sold appliances most of his career. Neither were what Arty would call go-getters but they brought in ad money in a dependable if plodding we-have-to-do-it-to-make-a-living sort of way.

At yet another table, all by himself, sat Howard Branigan, the Chief Engineer. He'd made no bones of the fact he was peeved that he'd been called all the way into town from the transmitter building for a 'silly meeting'.

Misty Lane entered. She was a burst of Spring, so vibrant, so lovely, all the guys followed her with their eyes.

Susie Q frowned.

Arty had solved the problem of having the whole staff present by bringing in a part-timer to work the board, a kid from the local community college who filled in for the announcers on the holidays and sometimes on weekends.

The staff chattered cheerfully until Arty cleared his throat. Hoss kept on whispering to Smoky, only his whispers were as loud as most people talked. He was telling one of his notorious jokes. This one had something to do with a Swedish masseuse. But even the beefy DJ shut up at the first words out of Arty's mouth.

"I've sold the station. I am no longer the owner. In a few moments the new owner will address you. I trust you'll give him the attention and respect he deserves so that---." Arty got no further. Everyone was talking at once.

"You did what?"

"Did I hear you right? You sold KCOW?"

"How could you, Art, without letting us know?"

"Are we all out of a job?"

The hubbub rose, and it was then that Cry Baby swaggered in, his crew in tow. The wiseguys fanned out along the walls and stood with their arms folded. A hush fell as the staff stared in considerable surprise at the men in dark suits.

"What the hell?" Larry Todd said.

"Who are these jaspers?" Duke Banner asked.

Cry Baby walked to the front and motioned for Arty Johnson to take a seat. He wanted to show them, right out of the gate, who was in charge. Clearing his throat, he began.

"Pay attention. I'm only going to say this once. I'm Mr. Scarvetti, your new boss. How I got this dump is none of your frigging business. All that matters is that from here on out you take your orders from me and only me. I sign your paychecks, so if you want to go on feeding your frigging faces and paying your frigging bills, you'll do as I frigging say." He paused to see how the little speech he'd whipped up was going over.

Not too well. Half the staff appeared to be in shock. The other half were offended.

Susie Q was the first to stir her bulk. "Listen here, mister. Just because you bought KCOW doesn't give you the right to talk to us like that."

"The Goodrich blimp speaks." Cry Baby put his hands on his hips. "Rights? You want to talk to me about rights? Okay, try this on for size. As your boss, I have the frigging right to fire your frigging ass right this frigging second if I frigging feel like it. If you want to go on working for me, you'll button those walrus lips of yours. The same goes for the rest of you."

Duke Banner stood and put a hand on Susie Q's shoulder. "That was no way to talk to a lady, pilgrim. Did you have to be so rude? A little tact goes a long way."

Cry Baby snorted. "First a sperm whale, now a midget. As for rude, this is how I am. If you can't take it, you're welcome to leave. No one is keeping any of you here." He gestured at the door. "Those who want to quit, now's the time."

"Are you serious?" Howard Branigan asked.

"There are going to be changes around here, people," Cry Baby said. "Big changes, in case you're wondering. We're number two, I understand, and as I told your former boss, I'm not the kind of guy who likes to be number two at anything. My first priority is to make this station number one. I have some ideas how to go about it and I'll be meeting with some of you to get your input."

That went over better.

Larry Todd raised a hand. "Will these changes affect the music? Are we going to stay Country?"

"Over my dead body," Cry Baby said. "From now on we'll play real music. Oh, we'll throw in some yodeling for the yokels, but yes, there will be changes to the music. Anything else?"

Sam Dowd wriggled his fingers. "What about sales? What will we do?"

"You'll go on selling whatever it is you sell," Cry Baby said, "only you'll sell twice as much of it as before or you'll be canned." He waited for more questions but no one had anything to say. "Okay, then. My door is always open. Just be sure you set up an appointment first with the chick at the front desk." He indicated his crew. "These are my associates, you might say. They make sure my wishes are carried out. Anything they tell you to do, you do it as if it came from my mouth."

Hoss's booming voice filled the room. "Pardner, I've got me a notion. All this talk of change. You all are part of some whopper of a conglomerate, am I right? A big corporation means big money. Can I take it for granted raises are in the works for all of us?"

"Sure," Cry Baby said. "You can also take it for granted I'm the tooth fairy." He wondered, as he often did, why so many mothers gave birth to morons. "I'm not no conglomerate, tubby. Think of this as a Family enterprise. As for more money, that depends on you. Make me happy and you'll roll in moola. Make me mad and you'll eat maggots in the desert."

At that juncture Smoky Williams pushed his flat-crowned hat back on his head and stood. "I don't reckon as I like you much, hombre. I'm quitting here and now."

CHAPTER FIFTEEN

Arty Johnson tried to get the DJ's attention but Smoky Williams wouldn't look his way. Which was too bad. Smoky had been with him longer than any of the others and was as reliable as sunrise. Arty didn't want to lose him.

"Give me my severance pay, mister," Smoky was saying, "and I'm out the door."

Cry Baby touched his chest. "You don't like me? Is that what you just said? I'm talking business here and you take it personal?" His jaw muscles twitched. "Severance pay, huh? Sure. Dill. Pretty Boy. Take Mr. Personal here down the hall and give him what he has coming."

Smoky hooked his thumbs in his belt on either side of a large silver buckle in the shape of a bald eagle. "If the rest of you have any horse sense, you'll do the same as me. This galoot ain't nothing but trouble. I feel it in my bones." Touching his hat brim to the ladies, he clomped out.

Pretty Boy and Dill were close behind. Neither had to ask Cry Baby what to do. His tone had said it all. Pretty Boy slipped a hand into a jacket pocket and palmed his brass knuckles.

In the break room, Cry Baby was thinking that maybe he'd laid it on a little heavy. He wanted these gumballs to toe the line but it wouldn't be too bright to have all of them skip out on him. He had enough to do without replacing the staff. Suddenly changing tactics, he smiled and spread his arms. "I think we're getting off on the wrong foot, people. Give the new arrangement a chance. Don't do like that hothead did and bail."

Down the hall, Pretty Boy opened the door to Cry Baby's office. "After you," he said to the cowboy.

In the break room, Cry Baby saw his employees perk up and fed them some more nice. "When I said this is a Family concern, I meant it. From now on think of us as one big family with me at the head."

In the office, Dill slipped in close behind Smoky Williams and gripped both his arms. The shocked DJ had time to exclaim, "What do you think you're doing?" Then Pretty Boy sank his brass knuckles into the pit of Smoky's stomach.

In the break room, Cry Baby was on a roll. "About all that name-calling I did. I know I get carried away but I don't mean anything by it."

In the office, Pretty boy hit Smoky Williams again and again, either in the gut or the ribs but not the face or anywhere it would show. Williams tried to break free of Dill but he was a sapling to Dill's redwood.

In the break room, Cry Baby liked how everyone was eating up the slop. "This is my first radio station. I admit I've got a lot to learn but I learn fast. I hope all of you will help out by keeping the hassles to a minimum. What do you say? Can we work together? Will you help me stomp the other stations into the dirt?"

In the office, Pretty Boy straightened. Smoky Williams was as limp as an empty sack. Dill let go and Williams fell to his knees. Groaning, he pressed his hands to his middle. Spit dribbled down his chin. He gasped when Pretty Boy grabbed him by the front of his Roy Rogers shirt.

"You listening? Good. You're to leave town and never

come back. If you don't, if you go to the cops or give us any grief, you'll disappear off the face of the earth."

In the break room, the staff were grinning and saying to one another that maybe the sale wasn't so bad and maybe the new owner would be a change for the better and wouldn't it be nice to kick KWIN's butt for once?

In the office, Dill hoisted Smoky Williams to his feet. Pretty Boy smoothed the Roy Rogers shirt and put the flat-crowned hat back on Smoky's head.

"We'll help you out to your car. Stand up straight and act normal. Try anything and we'll drag you back in here, and the next time we won't go as easy on you."

In the break room, Cry Baby was doing as his father always did when a new soldier was brought into the organization. He went from hick to hick, shaking hands. It amused him, how they lapped it up with a spoon. Even the blimp, Susie Q, welcomed him as if he were St. Peter come to escort her through the pearly gates.

Cry Baby finished and made for the door. Opening it, he looked back. "Think over everything I've told you. I won't be making changes for a day or so. Until then, carry on as before. Arty, you stay and soothe any fears they might have. Val, Switch, Wolfman, you're with me."

"I think that went really well, Mr. Scarvetti," the latter remarked as they headed down the hall.

"I don't need your hairy face up my ass cheeks, Vario," Cry Baby said. "But you're right. They took to it like babies to candy. So long as they fall in line, things will go smoothly."

"What if they don't, Mr. Scarvetti?"

"Need you even frigging ask?"

The staff waited until the men in the dark suits were

gone to swarm Arty Johnson like ants swarming a picnic spread. They besieged him with questions about the sale and the new owner.

Arty played it cagey, as Big Frank had instructed. "I was tired of the grind, is all. I met Mr. Scarvetti on one of my trips to Las Vegas and he showed an interest in buying me out. I put him off until now."

"What happened to your finger, Mr. Johnson?" Misty Lane asked.

Arty had forgotten about the splint. "I tripped. Had too much to drink and broke it when I fell." It reminded him of that terrible man in the Aviator shades who had snapped his pinkie as easily as he would snap a pencil. Anger flared, and he considered going to the police---for all of three seconds. On the ride to Yuba City, Lou Scarvetti had made it plain what would happen if he did. Arty remembered every word: "Mess with us and you'll be whacked. Your fucking wife will be whacked. Your fucking kids will be whacked. Your fucking mother, your fucking dog, your fucking cat, your fucking goldfish if you have one. You might get me thrown behind bars but you won't live out the week."

Arty believed him. He'd never had any dealings with criminals but he knew a psychopath when he met one. Louis Scarvetti had no scruples, no morals, no ethics. To Scarvetti, killing was on a par with brushing his teeth or combing his hair. Something that had to be done from time to time, and no big deal.

It scared Arty that men like the Scarvettis existed. He'd seen *The Godfather* years ago and kept abreast of the news. But it was one thing to read about a Mob hit in some faraway place like New Jersey and another to meet cold-blooded killers who actually did the---what had Scarvetti called it?---the whacking.

Misty Lane brought him back to the here and now with, "I don't know about anyone else but I'm willing to give the new owner a chance to prove himself. Who knows? Maybe it was a case of nerves that made him come across as so mean at first."

Hoss stroked his bushy red beard. "I suppose, gal. But there's something about those fellas that bothers me. I can't put my finger on what, exactly."

"I didn't like being called no midget," Duke Banner said. "Hell, he isn't much taller than me. And he had no call to say those terrible thing about our darling Susie."

The female DJ shrugged her dumpling shoulders. "That's all right, sugar. Don't get your dander up. I've been called worse." She fiddled with the fringe on her buckskin jacket. "Misty has the right notion, I reckon. We should give this hombre the chance to prove himself. If he works out, fine and dandy. If not, well, I've always had a hankering to try my luck in one of the bigger markets. Kansas City, maybe. Or Denver."

Misty turned to go, saying, "I guess I should get back to the phones."

Billy Holliday put a hand on her shoulder. "Did we get a call from the Fester brothers? I'm hoping they'll sign for a month's worth of spots in morning drive. I got Clem to agree to sponsor the eight a.m. news plus a full rotation from six until nine."

"*Take your hand off her.*"

Valentino was in the doorway. He didn't know it but at that instant he looked fit to kill. The sight of the salesman touching Misty Lane had triggered something in him. A feeling he'd never felt before, a feeling he shouldn't have given how briefly he'd known her. It shocked him almost as much as it shocked everyone else.

Billy Holliday jerked his hand away and shrank into his chair. "Sorry. I didn't mean anything."

"Mr. Corcione!" Misty exclaimed. "What was the meaning of that?"

"I just thought---," Val said sheepishly. He didn't go on. To get out of there with some shred of dignity intact, he explained, "Mr. Scarvetti sent me. He wants to talk to the Chief Engineer. After they're through, he wants to talk to the two guys from Sales."

"I'll be there in a couple of minutes," Howard Branigan said.

"He wants to see you now."

Howard Branigan seemed about to argue but he must have changed his mind because he stood and walked out.

No one uttered a peep until the pair were gone. Then Hoss whistled softly and asked, "What the dickens was that all about, honeypie? I swear, that young fella was riled something fierce."

"I honest to goodness have no idea," Misty said. But if anyone had peered closely at her, they might have noticed how her eyes twinkled.

Down the hall, Val was in a funk. He couldn't understand what had gotten into him. He was convinced he'd made a fool of himself. At Cry Baby's door he stopped and knocked. "In you go, Mr. Branigan."

As the engineer went in, Val glanced back down the hall. "What in God's name is happening to me?" he said under his breath.

CHAPTER SIXTEEN

Cry Baby pointed at a chair in front of his desk. "Have a seat. I hear you're the B.M.A.H."

"The what?" Howard Branigan said.

"Big Man Around Here." Cry Baby chuckled at his wit. "The one person the station can't do without. Arty tells me this place couldn't run without you."

"Stations don't run themselves," Howard said. "It takes years of education and training to keep a transmitter humming. So, yes, you could say I'm indispensable."

"Is that so?" Cry Baby liked an honest egotist. He could understand someone who thought they were hot stuff because he was hot stuff, himself. "Then maybe you can tell me, Mr. Indispensable, why my frigging station sounds like puke?"

Howard Brannigan was momentarily nonplused. He was more than competent at his job. He'd gone to Brown, majored in electronics, gotten his diploma, and worked as an assistant engineer at a station in Wyoming and another in Kansas before he applied to be Chief at KCOW. "What the hell are you talking about, mister? Our signal is crystal clear. I do calibrations daily, take field strength readings weekly, and my maintenance logs are always up to date."

"All that work you do yet KWIN sounds so much better than us."

Howard blinked. "I disagree. Our signal is as clear as theirs. It's just that, all other things being equal, they have a hundred thousand watt transmitter and we have a fifty thousand."

"What if we had a hundred thousand whatsis of our own?"

"I wish. We aren't licensed for it."

"So Arty told me. But could you install a new one if I got hold of it? A hundred thousand watt transmitter?"

Howard shook his head. "It's illegal for us to switch transmitters without FCC approval."

"Who's to know?" Cry Baby said, and winked. "I'm not going to tell anyone. Are you?"

"Are you for real?"

"Ten grand worth of real. That's how much I'll pay you to make the switch and to keep your mouth shut. Under the table, free and clear. What do you say?"

"Ten thousands dollars?"

"No, ten thousand Twinkies. Dumbass."

Howard Brannigan stared. He was thinking that the FCC would fine them silly. He mentioned as much, adding, "And where are you going to get the hundred thousand watt transmitter? Order a new one? That'll take months. But let's say you do find one and make the switch. Someone is bound to notice the change in our signal. The people at KWIN and KDLR, for starters. There will be an investigation. We'll be caught."

Cry Baby wasn't afraid of the Feds. He'd dealt with government bozos before. Nine times out of ten a bribe smoothed things over. The tenth time? That was what his crew was for. "You let me worry about that. I give you my word you won't be held to blame. But understand this. I'll get a new transmitter and I want it up and running by next week."

"Do you have any idea what you're asking?"

"Can it be done?"

"If I worked day and night, maybe," Howard said. "But why the big rush?"

"Arty tells me the ratings people will be calling households all over Yuba City next month or so, taking a poll for the next Blue Book, whatever the hell that is. With the new transmitter and the other changes I'm planning to make, we'll be number one."

"You're forgetting KWIN. They're not going to roll over. Their signal will still be as strong as ours, and they have damn good announcers."

"Let me worry about the competition. What I need to know, here and now, is whether you'll do the job?"

"I don't know. I suppose if you can get a hundred thousand watter, I could switch to our backup transmitter while I tear down the fifty thousand watter and install the new one."

"Wait a minute." Cry Baby sat up straight. "We have two transmitters?"

"Sure. Every station does. A main and a backup for when the main has to go off-line for repairs and whatnot. Our backup is a ten thousand watt tube job built back when records players were popular but it holds up."

"Does KWIN have a backup, too?"

"A fifty thousand watter." Howard sighed. "Sad, isn't it? Their backup is as powerful as our main. And that signal array of theirs. Their three towers are ideally located."

"Did you say towers?"

Howard was beginning to realize just how little the new owner knew about radio. "Yeah. You've seen radio towers before, I'm sure. Those tall spindly things with blinking lights that look like they were made from an Erector Set?"

"The only erections I know about are the kind that have to do with hookers."

"No. I'm talking abut the kits they make for kids to build stuff. I had one."

"I didn't. Let's stay on track here. Tell me more about these towers."

"Some stations have one, some two, some have three or more. The array depends on the coverage area. They're the one part of my job I don't like. Having to climb to the tops of the towers to replace bulbs. I'm not fond of heights."

"So you'll do the switch?"

"You're asking an awful lot, Mr. Scarvetti."

Cry Baby figured the engineer was hedging because he wanted more money. He didn't mind giving in, just this once, since there was no one else who could do the job. "What if I up it to fifteen grand?"

Howard licked his lips. The idea of illegally installing a transmitter was insane, but God help him, they were talking fifteen thousand dollars. "You did hear me say that the FCC will fine us up the ass?"

Cry Baby grinned. The son of a bitch was devious. He liked that. "Fifteen thousand and I pay all fines."

"You have a deal, Mr. Scarvetti," Howard Brannigan said.

They shook hands.

"I'll be talking to you soon about the new transmitter," Cry Baby told him."We'll probably get hold of it tomorrow night or maybe the next. Have your tools and stuff ready. My boys will help you but it will be strictly your show. Don't let me down."

Howard asked, "Is there any chance I can have the money in advance?"

"Don't push it,. You get the dough when the job is done and not before. Now go jerk off dreaming of what you can do with that much green." Cry Baby chuckled as the door closed, and laced his fingers behind his head.

He was pleased at how things were shaping up. Give him a month and he'd be the king of Yuba City radio. It would make his father proud. "Not bad for a beginner," he said aloud. "Maybe coming here wasn't such a bad idea, after all."

CHAPTER SEVENTEEN

Misty Lane usually got off work at five. Thanks to extra demands imposed by her new employer, today she didn't get done until almost seven. Most of the staff had already left. Duke was on the air until sign-off at midnight. Susie Q was in the production room recording commercials.

Mr. Scarvetti and his associates were bunkered in his office with two lawyers and a strange man who carried a ledger around. Doing what, Misty couldn't guess. Scarvetti had made a point of telling her that she wasn't to interrupt them for any reason whatsoever.

Misty was glad to be heading home. It had been a stressful day. It wasn't the change in ownership that bothered her, or that Smoky Williams had up and quit. No, what made the day stressful was the incident in the break room when poor Billy Holiday was threatened by Val. Misty couldn't stop thinking about it. She couldn't stop thinking about him.

Val. Valentino. How many times had Misty said his name in her head, rolling it on her mental tongue as if testing its flavor? How many times had she looked up from typing a letter or answering a call, only to see his face floating on the wall or on the ceiling next to Bessy, the KCOW mascot? Dear Lord, he was handsome. The handsomest man Mindy ever met. All that dark, curly hair, and those mysterious eyes were enough to make a girl's heart skip a beat.

Misty told herself she was being childish. They barely knew each other. Then, too, any man who would do what he'd done, growling at poor Billy Holiday for touching her, must be the jealous type. The kind who wouldn't let a woman so much as look at another man. The kind who beat their women. She could do without that, thank you very much. The smart thing for her to do was to stop daydreaming and have nothing more to do with him.

Her mind made up, Misty felt better than she had all afternoon. She pressed a stick-on memo to her desk top to remind her of a letter she must type first thing in the morning. Then she slid her purse strap over her shoulder, checked her hair in her compact mirror, and walked out, her high heels clicking on the hardwood floor.

A breeze fanned Misty's cheeks. It was a magnificent summer evening, the sky a turquoise blue sprinkled with fluffy clouds. She paused, debating whether to get a bite to eat or make her own supper.

"I've been waiting for you."

Startled, Misty spun. "Mr. Corcione." She suppressed her shock. "What are you doing there in the shadows? This makes twice you've scared the wits out of me. Please don't make it a habit."

Val wanted to kick himself. But if he'd waited by the door, he ran the risk of Cry Baby spotting him. "I had to see you."

"Oh?" Misty composed herself but inwardly she was in turmoil.

"I wanted to say how sorry I am for how I acted in the break room." Val exhaled the breath he hadn't realized he was holding. There, he'd gotten it out. So why was she staring at him as if he were Jack the Ripper? If she only knew the trouble he was letting himself in for by shirking his duty in order to talk to her.

An hour ago, Val had gone on an errand for Cry Baby. Eddy the Book needed to see some records pertaining to the ownership transfer, and Cry Baby tabbed him to drive Eddy to city hall and back. It was when they returned, when he saw Misty on the phone, that he'd decided to dare Cry Baby's wrath.

Val hadn't gone back into the office when Eddy the Book did. He'd lingered near the control room, watching the DJ. He knew Cry Baby was going to be tied up with Eddy and the lawyers for hours. After ten minutes had gone by and Cry Baby didn't bellow his name, he'd drifted outside to wait for Misty to get off.

Val had stayed out of sight as the station staff trickled home. He knew he was doing wrong. He should be in there with Cry Baby, as he'd promised Big Frank. But all he could think of was Misty and how he yearned to spend time in her company. It was ridiculous. Here he was, the guy who'd dated more women than Casanova, who'd scored more times than Babe Ruth, who could have any Vegas showgirl he wanted, and he was mooning over a country girl from a backwater town. Over a girl who'd never slept with a man. Who was saving herself for marriage. Who was an honest-to-goodness, hard-as-it-was-to-believe real life virgin.

Val had never met a virgin before. At least, none of the women he'd been with professed to being one or acted like they were. Then again, how was a virgin supposed to act?

It confused and unsettled him that he was so hot and bothered over Misty Lane. The waiting had given him time to think and review his feelings, and he'd decided he was infatuated. That was it. The same as seeing a new car and thinking you had to have it when you were just excited by all the chrome and polish and whistles. That was his problem. He was infatuated. All he had to do was wait and his feelings for her would fade.

But now, gazing into Misty's wonderful blue eyes, a flicker of doubt assailed him. Val had said he was sorry. He should go inside and rejoin the crew. Tearing his gaze from hers, he looked down at his feet and willed them to move toward the door. The traitors wouldn't budge. They were glued to the sidewalk.

"Is there anything else, Mr. Corcione?" Misty asked.

"No."

"I'll see you tomorrow."

Val drank in the enticing swirl of her hair and the alluring sway of her hips as she turned to walk way. Before he knew what he was doing, he had gripped her elbow and was saying, "Wait. Please. There is something else."

Misty waited, keeping her face blank, unwilling to let him know how affected she was by his touch and his amazing good looks.

"I've gotten off on the wrong foot, I know. I've given you the wrong idea about me and I'd be grateful if you'd let me set things right by allowing me to take you out to eat. My treat. What do you say?"

"I think I should go home." Misty went to pull away.

Springing in front of her, Val blocked her path. He had the awful insight that if he let her leave, they'd never be any closer than they were at that moment. He couldn't let that happen. He found he wanted to get close to her, as close as could be.

"Please move."

"I can't. I mean---." Val stopped.

"You're making no sense, Mr. Corcione."

Val touched her hand and was grateful when she didn't jerk hers back. "I'd be grateful if you'd say yes. I give you my word I'll behave." Val dropped his voice to a whisper. "Please, Misty."

"This is most irregular."

"What can it hurt? A meal and some talk? You can tell me about Yuba City and I'll tell you whatever you'd like to know about me."

Misty hesitated. Something told her that this hunk was a sharpie, the kind of guy who'd want a lot more if he thought he could get away with it. The smart thing was to go. Give Jesse Stillwell a call and invite him over to watch TV or sit on the porch swing. Instead, she said, "All right, Mr. Corcione. Just this one time. Where would you like to go?"

Val nearly laughed with relief. "I thank you from the bottom of my heart. And I keep telling you. It's Val. Not Mr. Corcione."

"*Burgers and Buns* is closest, Val."

"We got food there earlier, remember?" Val reminded her. "I was thinking somewhere classier. Somewhere they serve food on plates, not wrapped in paper." He abruptly realized that if Cry Baby were to glance out the office window, he'd see them. Without thinking he clasped Misty's hand and headed for the street.

Misty's instinct was to pull her hand free. He sure did take liberties. But she had to remember he was from the big city and big city boys, from what she'd heard, were forward. They took a lot for granted So long as he didn't get fresh, she figured she wouldn't say anything. She let him hold her hand.

"Have you thought of a place?" Val asked.

"How about Kentucky Friend Chicken? They have booths, and I love their cole slaw."

"Not classy enough. Somewhere with tablecloths. And waiters. Candles would be nice, too. A place where they sell wine."

Misty laughed. "My word. You sound as if you're taking me out to propose instead of grabbing a bite to eat."

Never in his whole life had Val blushed as deeply as he blushed then. "I just want someplace nice."

"Well, there's The Beef Eater. They have cow skulls on the walls and milk cans for seats."

Val didn't think cow skulls would quite fit the mood he was going for. "What's the best restaurant in town? The one where people like the mayor and bank presidents eat?"

"That would be The Radison. I've never eaten there but they say the food is served on china and you get three spoons. They have a chandelier imported all the way from France."

"Now you're talking." They were almost to the curb, and Val slowed. His car was in Vegas and Cry Baby would go ballistic if he took one of the limos. "Where can we catch a cab?"

"We can take my car but you have to pick somewhere else."

"Why?"

Misty debated how to explain. *The Radison* was special. It was the kind of place you went to with someone who meant the world to you, not on a casual date with a virtual stranger. But she didn't want to hurt his feelings so she said, "It would cost an arm and a leg and I refuse to let you pay that much."

"Money is no object," Val assured her, and patted his

pocket to be sure his wad was there. "Where are your wheels?"

"You're not listening."

Val resorted to the disarming smile that never failed to persuade the opposite sex. "Humor me. If nothing else, it'll give you something to talk about with your friends."

Misty bit her lip. Unknown to him, he'd struck a nerve. Ever since her friend Lucy Barnes bragged about being taken to *The Radison* on prom night, she'd dearly desired to go herself.

"Look. I know I'm way out of line. But it would mean a lot to me. I don't often go out with a lady like you." Val waited tensely for her answer.

Misty was flattered. "I wish I was wearing a better dress. The people who go there usually dress up."

Val smothered an impulse to whoop with glee. "Believe me, you look terrific as you are. Anyone says different will eat their teeth."

Misty assumed he was joking, and grinned. "You wouldn't really hit someone."

Of course Val would but he shook his head and gently squeezed her fingers. "Thank you for going. Which way to this buggy of yours?"

It turned out to be a white Dodge Neon with a manual transmission. In order to impress her, Val opened the door. He was amused by how she pressed her dress against her legs to keep it from hiking above her knees. Whistling cheerfully, he scooted around to the passenger side, half-afraid she'd change her mind and drive off before he got in. The interior was spotless.

"I've only had this a couple of months," Misty said. "It's the first car I ever bought on my own." She gripped the stick. "It's not much but it's my baby. One day I hope to afford a Corvette."

"Vettes are for people who like to drive fast."

Misty giggled self-consciously. "I have a confession to make. I have a heavy foot. Just ask my mom. She says I floored our riding mower when I did the lawn."

They laughed, and Val felt the tension drain from him like water from a sieve.

"It would be cool to cruise down the highway in a Corvette," Misty said. "The wind in my hair, nowhere to go, just driving for the fun of driving. Know what I mean?"

Val looked at her and a warm sensation spread through his chest. "Yeah, I do."

"Buckle your seatbelt." Misty squealed the tires as she angled into the street, then did what Val had never seen a girl do. She popped the clutch. In a Neon. They were at fifty in seconds. Misty grinned, her golden tresses flying in the wind from the open window. The hem of her dress had risen, revealing glimpses of creamy thighs.

Val's skin prickled all over, and without being aware of it, he licked his lips.

CHAPTER EIGHTEEN

"Tell me about yourself," Misty said, not taking her eyes off the road.

"Ladies first."

"There's not much to tell. I was born and raised on a farm six miles out of town. I went to grade school at Yuba Elementary. After that it was Yuba Middle School, then the ever popular Yuba High. I got fair grades. I was on the track and basketball teams. Oh, and I joined the Pep Club two years running."

"What's that?"

"We made posters and banners for games. Our motto was 'School Spirit is Contagious. Pass it on.' We entered a float in the Thanksgiving parade and it won an award for third place."

Val slid on the seat when she took a corner well over the speed limit. Working the shift as smoothly as a driver at the Indy 500, she held the Dodge to the center line. "Well?" he said.

"Well what?"

"That was it? Your whole life's story?"

"Sad to say."

"There has to be more. What about all the exciting things you've done? Vacations you've been on. Stuff like that."

"We went to San Francisco one summer. I saw Fisherman's Wharf and the Golden Gate Bridge. We also spent a few days in the redwoods. Does that count?"

"What else?"

Misty glanced at him, at those marvelous black curls and those dark eyes. "You don't get it, do you? There is nothing else. I'm a small town girl and I've lived a small town life. Excitement, for me, was the county fair each summer. Or winning second place in the hundred meter at a state meet. Or having one of my quilts on display at the church bee."

Val had heard there were people who lived her simple kind of life. It struck him that Misty and him came from two separate worlds. His childhood had been a slice of hell where he was lucky to get one square a day and never knew from one sunset to the next if he'd be alive to see the dawn. Her world was a slice of heaven, with a nice home and caring parents and a safe community.

"Is something wrong?"

"We're different, you and me."

"How so?"

"Our whole lives. Who we were. Who we are. If I told you some of the things I've done, you'd--." Val stopped. He was going to say, 'think I'm scum'. But he changed it to, "---think I'm not such a nice guy."

"What are you, an axe murderer?" Misty quipped. "You can't have done anything all that bad. I'd really like to hear about your life."

"Maybe later."

Misty glanced over. He had clenched his fists and a haunted aspect had come over his handsome face. Intuition told her it wasn't an act. He'd done something he was reluctant to share. It kindled her curiosity. "Whatever you think is best. I don't mean to pry. I just wanted to get to know you a little better." A lot better, a tiny voice at the back of her mind piped up, but she told it to shush.

"I'd like to get to know you, too."

An uncomfortable silence claimed them until Misty zipped into a curved drive fronting a building that Val swore he'd seen in *The Hunchback of Notre Dame.* Imposing, massive, it possessed the added distinction of being one of the highest buildings in Yuba City. The entrance was an elaborate arch wide enough for a limo to go through sideways. Above the arch blazed a sign: *The Radison Hotel.*

"I thought you said we were going to the best restaurant in town?"

"This is the place. It's on the ground floor. Everyone who is anyone comes here to eat. Everyone who can afford it, that is." Misty suddenly stiffened and tromped on the brakes.

A valet in a spiffy white jacket had materialized out of nowhere. Unfazed by his close call, he gave the Neon a look that said, 'You've got to be kidding me' as he stepped to the driver's side. "Park your car for you, ma'am?"

"That's okay," Misty said. She was accustomed to doing things herself.

Val climbed out and walked around. "I'll get that," he said as the valet reached for the driver's door. Opening it, he took Misty's hand and pulled her out. "Let doofus here park your baby. It's his job." Pivoting, he stopped the valet from getting in while simultaneously fishing out his wad. "Pay attention. I want it parked close to the entrance, not out near the street." He spotted an empty slot near the arch. "There will do."

"That's Mr. Hamblin's space."

"Who?" Val peeled off a twenty.

"You know. From Hamblin, Feinstein and Lieberman. If I let you park there I could get in trouble."

Val peeled off another twenty and wagged the bills under the guy's nose. "You didn't hear me? When I said there will do, I meant that's where you'll park it."

The valet glanced at the empty space, grinned, and snatched the bills. "On the other hand, I doubt he'll show up tonight. If he does, I'll just say another valet parked your car by mistake."

"Just so it's there when we come out," Val said. "If it's not, I'll break your fingers."

The valet laughed a little nervously. Sliding in, he whisked the Neon toward the slot, narrowly missing a departing Cadillac.

"That wasn't very nice, what you said to him," Misty remarked. Unlike the valet, she suspected that her Mystery Man was serious.

"I told you," Val said, looping his arm in hers and strolling toward the gilded glass doors.

"Told me what?"

"I'm not nice. I do things like that all the time. Just this morning I was in a bar fight with a bunch of bikers. I kneed one in the groin and jabbed another in the throat." Val braced for her reaction. That he was being so honest stunned him. But he couldn't seem to stop himself.

"Did you like doing that?"

"They were hurting a friend of mine. They got what they deserved."

Misty digested the revelation as a doorman admitted them. Preoccupied, she didn't realize the blunder she'd made until she saw the maitre d'. She stopped and clutched Val's arm.

"What's the matter?"

"I just remembered. We didn't call ahead. We don't have reservations and there's just no way anyone eats here without them."

"Is that so?" Val smiled and leaned close enough to nibble on her ear. "Watch a pro at work, sweet lady." He wasn't looking at her face and didn't see the quick glance she gave him or the color that crept into her cheeks. Taking a hundred from his wad, he folded it in the palm of his right hand.

The maitre d' poised a quill pen over a list. "And you are, sir?"

"Hungry." Val took his hand and pumped it.

The maitre d' looked at the bill and set down the pen. "Ah, yes. You have a reservation for two, I see. Right this way."

"I want somewhere private," Val said. "This is a special night. I'm treating the lady."

They wound up near the kitchen but that was okay because they had a booth to themselves. Val had the matre de bring a bottle of the best wine the hotel offered. The menu was royal purple, the print so small you needed a magnifying glass to read it, the prices outrageous.

Val didn't care. He had between three and four thousand dollars on him. Done making his selection, he straightened and was surprised to find his date giving him a funny sort of doe-eyed look. "What?"

"Nothing," Misty Lane said.

CHAPTER NINETEEN

"Where the hell is Valentino?"

Pretty Boy and Dill were the only wiseguys in the office. Pretty Boy was in front of the mirror, preening. Dill had unscrewed the lid on a pickle jar and was about to dip his fingers in. They looked at each other and then at Cry Baby.

"I haven't seen him in hours, Mr. Scarvetti," Pretty Boy said.

Dill thought a bit. "Me either, boss." He held out the jar. "Care for a pickle?"

"I hate those frigging things," Cry Baby said. "The only thing it would be good for is to shove it up your frigging ass." He didn't like it when one of his crew went missing. He never knew but it might be enemy action. A rival Family, the cops, the Feds, they'd all love to get their hands on one of his soldiers in the hope of extracting information that would bring him down. Since it was unlikely the other Families knew he'd left Vegas, he chalked them off as suspects. And if the cops or the Feds were to blame, he'd find out soon enough. Thanks to the Supreme Court, everyone had the right to a phone call. All he had to do was wait.

He hated waiting.

Cry Baby stood and stretched. He was beat. But he'd gotten a lot done and laid plans for a lot yet to do. Before another week was over, his radio station would be the undisputed best in Yuba City. Number one. Wait until pops hears about it, he thought with pride.

Cry Baby glanced at a memo from the bimbo. The mayor wanted to get together.

Apparently word of the change in ownership was spreading and Yuba City's bigwigs were eager to check him out. In addition to His Honor, two bankers, three city councilmen and several members of the chamber of commerce had phoned.

Cry Baby liked being courted by the shakers and makers. Maybe Yuba City was a small pond compared to Vegas but small ponds had their big fish and their little fish and he liked being one of the biggest. Especially since, for once, no one was looking over his shoulder. No one was telling him what to do. He could strut his stuff, show his father what he was made of.

Cry Baby was well aware his old man had doubts about his ability to take over the Family. Here was a chance to put those doubts to rest, to prove he had what it took.

Contemplating the schemes he'd cooked up, Cry Baby smiled. They were worthy of the legends of yore, worthy of Capone and Marciano and those kinds of guys. Worthy, even, of the Mafiosos in the films he loved so much, the films his father always ragged him about.

Cry Baby didn't understand why his father got so bent out of shape. Some of the movies were great. His favorites were those with his idol, Al Pacino. He'd watched *The Godfather* and *Scarface* so many times, he had the lines memorized.

That Pacino. He was the kind of wiseguy Cry Baby could relate to, the kind he'd always wanted to be. Pacino didn't take guff off of anybody. Cry Baby particularly loved that scenes where Pacino offed somebody. Pacino alwawys did it with style, with flair. Cry Baby ate it up.

His father was always going on about how it was make-believe. How moves were 'just' movies. His father missed the point. So what if they were movies? They showed how things should be. Al Pacino was the coolest and toughest movie Mob guy ever. What harm was there if Cry Baby couldn't get enough of watching him in action? Everybody should have a hero.

Shaking himself, Cry Baby came back to the here and now. "We're leaving," he announced.

"Where are we going, boss?" Dill asked.

"To a hotel I heard about." Cry Baby had done some asking around. According to the hickweeds, one joint in town was head and shoulders above the rest. *The Radison*, it was called.

He stopped at the front desk, wincing at the music that came from the speakers. It sounded like a cow was being strangled. He would take another day of this crap and then his changes would go into effect. The days of listening to hemorrhaging heifers on KCOW were about over.

Switch and the Wolfman were out in front of the station, the Wolfman taking a smoke. He ground it against the building as Cry Baby emerged.

"Either of you know where Valentino got to?"

The Wolfman shook his head. "I sure don't, Mr. Scarvetti."

Switch had an idea but he didn't share it. He'd noticed Val giving the blond bombshell strange looks. For his friend to show an interest in a foxy babe was nothing new. For Val to act so bent out of shape about it was.

"Screw him, then," Cry Baby said. "When he shows up

and finds us gone, he can track us down. And he'd better have a damn good excuse for his vanishing act."

The crew made for the street, two soldiers in front of Cry Baby, two soldiers behind him.

Switch and the Wolfman were almost to the curb when a red sports car squealed to a stop behind the limos. Switch streaked a hand to his special vest. The Wolfman moved between the sports car and Cry Baby, prepared to sell his own life to save Big Frank's son.

Out of the sports car hurtled a woman, a short, stout bundle of fury who stormed toward them like a female rhino on the rampage. Black hair framed an oval face that under calmer circumstances would be attractive. She wore a skimpy green dress that showed too much of her wide thighs. "Which one of you sons of bitches do I talk to?"

Switch looked at her in bewilderment. "What are you talking about, lady?

"As if you don't know," she snapped, her eyes spitting fire.

"Do you want something?"

"Damn straight I do." The woman tilted her neck to glare past Switch at Cry Baby. "It's you, isn't it? I can tell you're in charge." Shaking her purse, she shoved the Wolfman out of her way. "I want to know what in hell is going on."

Cry Baby was under the impression she was going to tear into him. "Hold on, sweetcheeks. I don't know who you are or what has your panties in a knot, but you must be making a mistake."

"Like hell. You're Louis Scarvetti, aren't you? The man who supposedly bought my husband's station?"

Cry Baby squared his shoulders. "So that's what this is about. There's no supposedly about it, lady. It's a done deal.

KCOW is mine." She cocked a fist and Cry Baby raised his own. She had spunk, this broad, and something else, something that made him think he knew her from somewhere. But no, he never forgot a face. He'd never laid eyes on her before.

"How much did you pay for it?"

"That's private information," Cry Baby answered, and was shocked when she lunged and grabbed him by the front of his shirt.

"Think again, bastard. KCOW was as much mine as it was Arty's. Maybe it wasn't down on paper but I worked as hard as he did to make it a success."

"Maybe you did." Cry Baby was racking his brain to remember her name. Arty had mentioned it once. "Meriam, isn't it? I don't see what any of that has to do with me. Hasn't your husband explained the situation?"

Meriam Johnson let go. "That fucking douche won't tell me a fucking thing. All he'll say is that he sold it. When I ask how much he got, and where the money is, he clams up. Something is fucking strange here, mister, and I want to know what the fuck it is."

Cry Baby liked her. She used the f-word almost as much as he used to. She also had humongous hooters.

"I slapped the stupid fuck around and he still won't tell me," Meriam was saying. "So I came to see you. I want to know the truth, handsome. Or so help me, I'll make your fucking life so fucking miserable, you'll wish you were fucking stillborn."

"Did you just call me handsome, sweetcheeks?" Cry Baby was flattered but he couldn't let anyone talk to him the way she was doing. Not in front of his crew. "Tell you what. How about you and me go have a talk in my office.

Just the two of us." She immediately stomped past him. He turned to follow her and thought to say to his soldiers, "Stay put. This shouldn't take long."

CHAPTER TWENTY

Meriam Johnson didn't stop until she was in the office. She held the door for Cry Baby, then slammed it shut.

"All right, mister. Give it to me straight."

Cry Baby hit her. He drove his fist into her gut and stepped back to watch her collapse. Only she didn't. She recoiled a step, hissed between her teeth, and punched *him* in the gut. Cry Baby staggered. He brought up his fists to tear into her, and it was well he did, because she tore into him, flailing with her fists and her purse. There had to be an anvil in the thing because when it clipped him on the chin he nearly went down. Before he could recover she was on him, a madwoman gone berserk.

It was humiliating.

A snarl tore from Cry Baby's throat. He had a thing about being struck. His father and mother never hit him and he'd be damned if he's let anyone else, particularly this psycho bitch. He jolted her with a jab, then clamped his fingers on her throat. Battling, they turned from side to side. Somehow or other they collided with a chair and fell.

Meriam's fingers found Cry Baby's neck. Screeching like an alley cat, she sought to strangle him even as he tried to strangle her.

They rolled back and forth, neither doing real harm, and crashed into the desk. It brought them to a stop.

Cry Baby was on top, buoyed by her enormous melons, his right leg between her thighs. Her dress was up around her waist, exposing the tops of her nylons. She snarled, her eyes boiling with fury, her nostrils flared. Her lips were parted and her teeth were bared as if she were going to bite him.

Cry Baby couldn't say what made him do what he did next. By rights he should have beaten her silly, or at least slapped her around so she knew who she was messing with. Instead, he kissed her. He lowered his mouth and hungrily devoured hers, rimming her lips with his tongue.

Meriam Johnson stopped trying to kill him. Her body softened and she said, "What the hell? Why did you do that?"

Cry Baby could think of several reasons. The heat she gave off aroused him. Her near-naked legs aroused him. Her hooters aroused him. Then there was their fight. He liked it rough, liked babes who didn't mind being smacked around ,and gave as good as they got. To his surprise, he realized something else. Meriam looked a lot like his mother. He didn't tell her that. He said, "Because you're smoking hot."

Meriam gazed into his eyes. "Who the fuck are you, Scarvetti? Where do you come from? How did you steal the station out from under my incompetent fucking husband?"

Rising to his knees, Cry Baby smoothed his jacket, then her dress. He deliberately ran his hand along her inner thigh as he did. "You want answers, hot momma? Okay, I'll give you answers. But there's a catch."

Meriam stared at the bulge in his crotch.

"Be here tomorrow night, say about eleven," Cry Baby said. "Wear something sexy, something that shows off those great tits of yours, and I'll tell you all you want to know. Only you might not like what you hear." He held out a hand to help her up and she took it.

Meriam pressed against him, her breath warm on his neck. "Are you planning to seduce me, Mr. Scarvetti?"

Cry Baby thought he'd explode then and there. "Lou. Call me Lou. You're a grown woman. You figure it out." He gestured at the door but she gripped his shoulders and mashed her mouth against his. Man, she could kiss.

Cry Baby figured that was the end of it but she gripped his manhood, smiled, and left. Just like that. No more name-calling. No raving.

"Man, that is one loony broad," Cry Baby said.

Meriam Johnson was a woman who knew what she wanted out of life and how to go about getting it. 'It' being financial security. Enough money to do as she pleased from day to day, and to comfortably retire on later. That was why she'd married Arty Johnson.

Her maiden name was Marchand. She was born in St. Louis. Her father moved to Yuba City to take a job at the tire plant when she was fourteen. After life in a real city, life in a town that called itself a city but was still only a town was dull, dull, dull.

There was an upside, though. Meriam had discovered the joys of liplocks before the family moved, which made her popular at Yuba High. It also helped that in her younger and admittedly slimmer days, she was eye candy. Sensual as all get-out, so sexy that half the guys at Yuba City High had a crush on her. She could take her pick. The star quarterback, the class president, the handsomest boy in the class, they all panted after her. She set her sights on Arty Johnson.

At the time it seemed like the smart thing to do. Arty's family had money. Not millions but more than most in Yuba City. He took business courses all through high school and managed straight A's.

When Meriam first bumped into him---literally---she thought he was going to have a stroke. He'd gawked and fumbled with her books and mumbled like he had cheese dip crammed in his mouth. Getting him to fall for her was as easy as puckering her lips.

Later, it was her brainstorm to invest in the radio station. It put them in debt but it promised to pay off in the long run. When they were ready to retire, they could sell KCOW for ten times what they paid for it. In the meantime, their income wasn't great but more than enough by Yuba City standards.

Subsequent events justified Meriam's decision. The star quarterback became a drug addict and a wreck. The class president was a sanitation engineer. And the handsomest guy in their class was living with another handsome guy in San Francisco.

Arty turned out to be the best catch, except for a few flaws. The Lord knew, Meriam didn't like to nag, but how could she not when her husband was such a wuss? He let everyone push him around. When they first bought the station, he'd let the staff do pretty much as they pleased, even going so far as to ask them what they thought they should be paid.

Meriam put a stop to his nonsense. She became the power behind the microphone, as it were. Arty had the mistaken notion that their marriage was a fifty-fifty proposition but he was kidding himself. She made the major decisions while manipulating him into thinking her ideas were his.

Then there was their so-called love life. Simply put, Arty made love like a sponge. That is to say, he laid there like a flabby lump while she did all the work. She was the one who had to light his fuse and keep it burning.

In the early days Meriam didn't mind all that much. Screwing was screwing, she'd deceived herself into thinking. What did it matter who was in the saddle? It mattered a lot, eventually. Meriam grew tired of faking orgasms rather than having them.

One day Arty hired a studly announcer from Oklahoma. Thinking about the guy's tight jeans and hard butt made Meriam horny enough to hump a doorknob. One evening in the production room she humped him, and he produced nicely. Unfortunately, four months later her lover's mother came down sick and he flew back to Tulsa to look after her. Who would have thought someone so manly was a momma's boy?

Meriam went on with her life. She considered divorce for a while but after wasting twenty years with Arty, she wasn't about to throw in the towel when in another ten they'd sell the station, move to Arizona, and live in cozy comfort the rest of their days. It was conceivable they might get as much as five million, enough to make those wasted years worth her while.

Then this happened.

Arty had gone on one of his jaunts to Vegas. Meriam didn't think much of it. She let him go now and then because it gave her time to herself. She knew he gambled but she'd made it plain he wasn't to go overboard. She also knew he fooled around but she was having fun, too.

The moment Arty walked in the door after this last

trip, Meriam sensed something was wrong. He had that look, the look he always got when she caught him doing something he shouldn't, like a puppy that knows it's in for a beating. She'd ragged on him for hours before he revealed the horrible truth.

The jackass had sold the station.

Meriam slapped him from one end of the house to the other, using language that would shame a trucker.

She'd tried her best to pry the details out of him but for once in his life Arty showed grit. He refused to open up, refused to tell her much. So she'd gone to the station to confront Scarvetti.

Now, driving home, Meriam tried to piece together the puzzle. A few things were self-evident. If Scarvetti was a broadcaster, she was a nun. He looked more like a hood than an executive. An Italian hood. As for the guys in the dark suits, she was at a loss. Or was she? The way they'd acted when she drove up, she'd bet the few thousand she had squirreled away that they were his bodyguards. An Italian hood plus four protectors. That spelled the Mob. Surely not, she told herself. Surely even Art wouldn't be stupid enough to get involved with the Mafia?

She recalled how hungrily Scarvetti kissed her. She couldn't forget the bulges, either. Not the bulge in his pants but the bulges under each arm. She'd felt them when they grappled. Pistols in shoulder-holsters, unless she missed her guess.

The conclusion was inescapable. It sparked all kinds of questions, questions her mouse of a husband was going to answer when she got home.

She had a question of her own to wrestle with, too. If her hunch proved right, what was she going to do about it? Run to the police? The Mafia didn't like it when people did that. The people ended up dead.

Then there was her meeting with Scarvetti tomorrow night. Should she go or no? What he had in mind was obvious. She wasn't offended. She had to confess she found him stimulating. Meeting him on the sly might prove to be rewarding. She'd get to know him better, perhaps find a weakness she could exploit.

Meriam must be careful, though. Scarvetti wasn't a wimp, like Arty. He was an animal. He was also a man, and men, by and large, were simpleminded Neanderthals ruled by that thing below their belts. A clever female could get most any man to eat out of her hand.

Meriam smiled. Where most women would be in tears or on the verge of a breakdown, she was excited. For the first time in decades she wasn't bored. Life had thrown a challenge in her face and she would rise to meet it as she rose to meet every challenge. Whatever that idiot Arty had done, she could undo.

One way or the other.

CHAPTER TWENTY-ONE

At that exact moment Cry Baby was in the back seat of his limo listening to a CD collection of the greatest singer of all time. "My baby said good-bye-ye-ye. My-oh-my. My baby didn't cry. Why, oh why?" The chorus came on and Cry Baby joined in. "My baby don't cry. My baby don't cry."

In the front seat Switch glanced at Pretty Boy, who was driving. "You'd think a cat was being killed," he said so only Pretty Boy heard.

At one time both of them liked Frankie Valli and the Four Seasons. That was before Cry Baby got hold of every song the group put out and listened to them hour after hour, singing along as if he were Frankie. It gave them a whole new appreciation for ear plugs.

Dill and the Wolfman had it worse. They were in the middle seat, facing Cry Baby.

The Wolfman wished he could interest Cry Baby in Mozart or Bach. He'd tried once. Cry Baby's response? "I don't listen to dead guys from other countries."

The song came to an end.

Switch braced for *Sherry* but Cry Baby had him pop out the CD and pass it back, then turned on the dome light and examined it.

"Is it scratched or something, Mr. Scarvetti?"

"Pen and paper, quick," Cry Baby said, snapping his fingers.

Dill was sucking on his namesake. He patted his pockets and said with his mouth full, "I donth goth any."

The Wolfman produced a notepad and a ballpoint. "Here you are, Mr. Scarvetti."

Cry Baby placed the pad on his knee and was about to write when the limo wheeled into a curved driveway. An ornate building reared, ablaze with lights.

"The Radison," Pretty Boy announced, slowing. He made for a row of empty parking spaces.

As a precaution they never, ever, let a valet park their vehicle. Self-preservation overruled laziness. A few years ago in the Big Apple, a capo let a valet park his car at an eatery and paid for it by being blown into fragments. Police later learned the valet was a hitman hired by an enemy.

Pretty Boy braked in an area under some trees, shifted into Park, and reached for the ignition key. He happened to glance at the entrance and blurted, "I'll be damned. Do you see what I see?"

They all looked.

Strolling casually out of The Radison arm-in-arm were Valentino and Misty Lane. They only had eyes for each other, and as Cry Baby and the wiseguys stared in surprise, Val brushed a stray strand of hair from Misty's forehead.

Cry Baby's temper erupted like a volcano. He snatched at the door handle to fling the door open. "That damn Corcione. Here I was worried about him and loverboy is out with the blonde bimbo. And he didn't even ask my permission."

Switch didn't want his friend to get into trouble. Thinking fast, he said with a laugh, "That's our Val. He sure doesn't waste time, does he, Mr. Scarvetti?" Switch nudged

Pretty Boy, and winked. "Can you believe that guy? We're not in town half a day and already he has a babe hanging onto him like she can't get enough."

Pretty Boy blinked and nodded and said, "Yep. That's our Val, all right."

"He's something else," the Wolfman threw in.

"She sure is a hottie," Dill contributed.

Cry Baby hesitated. Like the rest of them, he took pride in Valentino's exploits. Every time Val scored, it was like they did. They were in awe of his success, and liked to brag on him at wiseguy meets. A couple of years ago they'd tried to keep count but lost track at around one hundred and something. "I've heard of guys who were sunstruck and windstruck," Cry Baby said, "but Val is the first guy I ever met who's pussystruck."

The whole crew cracked up.

Cry Baby let go of the door handle.

"Want me to give him a yell, Mr. Scarvetti?" Dill asked.

Cry Baby had half a mind to call Val over and ream him out, really twist the screws. But his crew was eyeing their friend with envy.

Cry Baby did something he rarely ever did. He decided to be nice. "No. Leave them be. Loverboy can't make it through a night without getting his rocks off. But when he shows up tomorrow, I'm putting him straight on a few things."

"Whatever you think is best, Mr. Scarvetti," Switch said.

CHAPTER TWENTY-TWO

Hours earlier.

Misty Lane felt like a princess being courted by a dashing prince.

They hadn't been seated two minutes when Val snagged the sleeve of a waiter and smacked a twenty into his palm. "This is how it is. There's a lot more for you when we're done provided you wait on us hand and foot. I so much as wiggle my pinkie, I want you front and center. Any problems with that?"

"No, sir, none at all," the waiter said, and grinned greedily. "You'll have my special attention."

"Good. First thing is a candle in the middle of our table. And a vase of flowers if you can find one."

"Will plastic flowers do?"

"If you can't get real ones. I want this to be romantic. Got me?"

"I'm on it." The waiter scurried off.

"Romantic?" Misty repeated. She'd suspected how he felt about her but she never figured he'd be so blatant about it.

Val didn't reply. He had come to a decision. He was going all out to woo her. He had to. The odds were stacked against him. For starters she already had a boyfriend. Second, he might never get to go out with her again. She might refuse, or the boyfriend might raise a stink.

Then there was Cry Baby. Usually Cry Baby let his

crew do pretty much what they wanted where their love lives were concerned. But maybe Cry Baby would decree that the crew and the station staff weren't to fraternize. Or maybe Cry Baby would get the hots for Misty, himself. Either scenario, Val was screwed.

As if all that weren't enough, Val had the wild card factor to deal with, namely, her parents. Could be, they wouldn't like their daughter dating an Italian. Could be, they were fundamentalists who'd bristle at their pride and joy dating a Catholic. Not that he ever went to church. But her parents might be the kind who were hardnosed about something like that.

All these factors convinced Val that if he was to act, he must act now. He poured on the Corcione charm. He told nice clean stories and nice clean jokes, strictly PG stuff, stuff Disney would approve of.

Misty was fascinated. Through his eyes she saw the Windy City in all its facets. She walked with him along the breezy shore of Lake Michigan. She visited the Lincoln Park Zoo and the planetarium. The Botanical Gardens interested her immensely. Val had seen so much and done so much that after a while Misty got to thinking about how little she'd seen and done, and she grew sad.

"Am I boring you?" Val instantly asked.

"Not at all." Misty stared at the candle's dancing flame. "It's just that I envy you. I've only ever been out of Yuba City a few times. I have no idea what the rest of the world is like."

"It's not all it's cracked up to be." Val thought of his life on the streets, of the muggings, the knife fights, the killings. He thought of the pimps and the pushers and thirteen-year old streetwalkers and ten-year olds hooked on crack. He remembered a homeless man set on fire by punks with nothing better to do, and a woman who had her throat slit after she stumbled on a drug deal. He shuddered at the thought of any of that befalling a girl like Misty.

"You look upset?" Misty noticed.

"Not at all," Val mimicked her. He liked how sensitive she was to his moods, just as he was to hers. "I was thinking that you're better off not having seen some of the things I have."

"For instance?"

"I'd rather not talk about it."

Misty reached across and placed her hand over his and squeezed. "Don't hold back on my account. I told you all there is to know about me. I'd like to hear everything that made you, you."

"No," Val said, more gruffly than he intended. He feared that once she learned the truth, she wouldn't want anything more to do with him.

Misty sensed that despite what he said, deep down he had an urge to open up. She ran a finger along his hand. "Do it for me."

Val gazed into her wonderful eyes, and was lost. He couldn't imagine denying her anything. So be it. He took a deep breath. He would tell her the truth and nothing but the truth, and if she despised him afterward, then they were never meant to grow any closer than they were at that moment.

Misty prodded him with, "How awful can the life of a broadcast executive be, anyhow?"

"I'm not a broadcaster."

"Then what are you?"

"A wiseguy."

"You mean like a smart-aleck? How can you do that for a living?"

"God," Val said. He looked at her, at her angelic face, dazzled by the halo of innocence she radiated, and a lump formed in his throat. Raising her hand to his lips, he kissed a knuckle and stroked it. "I could easily fall in love with you," he said softly.

Misty's impulse was to pull her hand away. He was taking liberties again. The only thing was, she liked the liberties he was taking, liked them a lot. Decorum spurred her to say, "You can't be serious. We've only just met."

"How long must you know someone to care for them?" Val wasn't asking her opinion so much as voicing aloud the question uppermost on his mind.

"I don't know," Misty said. Not long at all if the warmth budding inside her was any indication. To change the subject she asked, "What's a wiseguy? What kind of work do they do?"

"A wiseguy is a made man," Val said. "I do whatever the man I work for wants me to do." He lowered his voice so no one at the other tables would hear. "Once I broke the wrist of an old geezer, a bookie who skimped on a few G's. Another time, a drunk at a night club made the mistake of sitting at my boss's table and wouldn't give it up when we got there so I hit him in the mouth and broke his teeth."

"I don't understand," Misty said. "Why would you do such terrible things?"

"Because that's the kind of work I do."

"Are you trying to shock me or something! Are you making this up?"

"Do you really think I'd be so childish?"

Misty gazed into his eyes. She saw his true feelings as

plainly as she could see her own hand in his. She saw something else, too, a terrible torment, and more than a trace of fear. It bewildered her.

Val girded himself. He was about to break the cardinal rule. "I'm in the Mafia, Misty."

"The Mafia? Like in the movies? That Mafia?"

"One and the same."

To Misty, the notion was as alien as life on the moon. She found it hard to accept there were people who went around hurting others. It was so---mean. "Do you like what you do? Do you intend to do it the rest of your life?"

"Until now I never gave it much thought," Val admitted. He stroked her hand some more. "But no, I wouldn't do it if you didn't want me to."

Misty's tummy roiled. She was moved but it was too much, too soon. "You don't know what you're saying."

Val had to cough before he could continue. "I know I'm way out of line, talking to you like this. Most guys date for months or years before they spill their guts like I'm spilling mine. And a wiseguy should never, ever, talk about what he does. But I can't help it. I think I'm falling for you and it scares me because I haven't fallen for anyone in so long, I've forgotten how."

"Opening our heart is like breathing," Misty said, her own emotions in a whirl. "We just feel it." A voice in her head warned her to pull her hand away but she let him go on holding it.

Val's vision blurred and his head swam. He became angry at himself. Here he was, acting like a stupid love-struck teenager. He'd been out with tons of women, gone to bed with more than he could count. Tall ones, short ones, brunettes, redheads, blondes, you name it. What made Misty Lane so special, he wondered, that he was falling apart like this?

The answer, Val realized, was right in front of him. It was Misty, herself. She was as different from the women he normally went out with as, say, a Girl Scout from a streetwalker. Misty was a babe, all right, but not that kind. She was as sweet as a newborn. She'd never harmed another soul her whole life. Deep down where it counted, she was a good person. In short, she possessed all the qualities he thought had long since gone extinct from the human race.

Plus Misty was a *virgin*.

CHAPTER TWENTY-THREE

Virginity.

To some people that wouldn't count for much. They'd laugh Misty to scorn and say she was being foolish for believing as she did. They'd call her dumb for saving herself for the man she would marry.

Val flattered himself that he understood. She wasn't doing it because she was scared to give her body or because she didn't have the same urges as everyone else. She was saving herself as a gift for the one who claimed her heart.

Val had never thought of sex as anything special. To him, sex had always been, well, 'sex'. Making whoopie was done for making whoopie's sake. It was sort of like eating. You ate because you were hungry. You had sex because you were horny. Climaxing was a bodily function, like taking a leak. To regard sex as special was a new concept. A startling concept, in that it implied there were other ways of looking at a lot of things.

Such as love.

All the foxy mommas Val had bedded, and never once was he in love. He never gave love a thought. Why should he? What love had he ever known? His father abandoned him, his mother cared for the bottle more than she cared for him. Until Big Frank came along, no one had showed him a lick of kindness, and even Big Frank's generosity had an ulterior motive behind it. As Val later learned, Big Frank was always on the lookout for guys with potential, guys who would make dependable soldiers. Yeah, Big Frank saved him from a life on the streets, but only to add a wiseguy to the Scarvetti ranks

It was no wonder Val had decided 'love' was dead, just like God was supposed to be. 'Love' was the stuff of fairy tales, of romance books, of soap operas and TV movies of the week. He'd firmly believed that 'love' didn't exist in the real world.

Then along came Misty.

When Val looked at her, he felt warm and caring. He was being stupid, part of him said. But another part said no. Another part said that his feelings for her were the truest he'd ever felt.

Now, grasping Misty's hand and meeting her frank gaze, Val let down his guard. He began to tell her about his past, and once he started, he couldn't stop. He told her everything, from the cradle to *The Radison*. He left nothing out. An inner dam had sprung a leak and a torrent gushed from his soul. He couldn't plug the leak if he tried. If he even wanted to try, which he didn't. He was glad to spill his guts, especially glad to spill his guts to her.

Misty listened, never saying a word. She didn't badger him with questions. She didn't judge him. She sat and listened. To his shattered childhood. To the nightmare of his life on the street. To the night Big Frank came into his life. To how he'd beaten dozens of deadbeats and done other terrible things at Big Frank's bidding.

Val related the time he took part in a hit. A Jamaican posse tried to muscle in on Big Frank's territory and Big Frank sent Cry Baby to deal with their leader. True to form, Cry Baby took a baseball bat to the Jamaican's skull. Pretty Boy and Dill held him while Cry Baby swung and swung.

Val waited out in the getaway car.

The Jamaicans didn't learn their lesson. In retaliation they snuffed a Family-connected shylock.

Big Frank unleashed the Iceman on them, and that was that. Legend had it the Iceman eliminated eleven of them inside of a month.

Val told Misty all this, and more. His cheeks burning, he mentioned his sexual escapades. He told her of his rep, told her about the showgirls and how it earned him his nickname, Valentino, after the cinema lover of yesteryear.

Val talked until he was nearly hoarse. He told her all there was to tell. More than he'd ever told anyone. When he was done he fell silent and waited for her to say he was scum. Waited for her to stand up and walk out. Waited for her to do what any decent girl would do.

Misty was in a daze. He'd thrown so much as her, it was overwhelming. At first she was dumfounded anyone could live as he did. Then she was horrorstruck that he'd suffered as he had. The longer he went on, another kind of horror gripped her. For a few brief minutes she regarded him as some sort of beast, a violence-prone brute she was better off avoiding.

Then it hit her. There they were, seated across from each other. Their hands were touching. He was flesh and blood. A real human being. Nothing less, nothing more.

That was what changed her mind.

As Misty continued to listen, she realized that here was someone barely older than she was, who had been through hell through no fault of his own. Val wasn't to blame for his father leaving their family or for his mother drinking herself to death. As for living on the street, he'd only done what he needed to in order to survive.

The same with being a wiseguy. As best Misty could understand, it was sort of like joining a fraternity. Or better yet, being blood brothers, the ritual kids did where they cut their fingers or their wrists and smeared blood. Only in the Mafia's case, they shed blood. A whole lot of it.

Misty compared Val to Jesse Stillwell. They were about the same age but there any resemblance ended. Val was worldly, a product of the cities. Jesse had been born and raised on a farm. Like her, Jesse hadn't seen much of the outside world. Like her, Jesse's life was made up of family and friends, people who were her friends, too, people they'd known since they were knee-high to a calf.

Michael Corcione's world was different. Theirs was light, his was dark. Theirs was peaceful, his was violent. Her minister would say his was evil, and maybe it was, but did that make Val evil? Should she get up and leave? A sensible woman would. A woman with any sense would refuse to have anything more to do with him.

Misty pulled her hands from his. The hurt that leaped into his eyes hurt her as well. He thought she was going to go. But she wouldn't. Not that she couldn't. She wouldn't, not after he'd bared his heart, and in the baring revealed that deep down where it mattered, he wasn't evil. He wasn't a brute. He was a young man Fate had dealt cruel blows. Had he been raised on a farm like Jesse Stillwell, she wouldn't think twice about going out with him.

Val saw the pink tip of her tongue wet her rosy lips. She was going to speak. She was going to crush the life from him with one word: "Goodbye". He'd bared all he was and she was going to kick him in the teeth and walk out of his life. He braced for the worst.

"Shouldn't we order some food? I'm famished."

"Food?" Val shook his head to clear it. It was odd how her voice drifted to him as if from the far end of a tunnel.

"That *is* why we came here, isn't it? To eat supper?"

Molten lava filled Val's chest and his tongue seemed to glue itself to the bottom of his mouth.

"Are you all right?"

Happiness welled. Happiness so potent, Val felt giddy. It was like being drunk, like downing a fifth of whiskey and feeling everything was right with the world. He laughed for joy. "Thanks to you I could flap my arms and fly."

"I'd rather you didn't. Everyone would stare."

They both laughed, and gazed at one another, their faces shining, so transparent that nearby patrons noticed and grinned.

Val didn't care. He didn't care about anything at all at that exact moment except for the woman across from him.

A memory flashed into his head. From back shortly after he became a wiseguy. He and several others were with Big Frank in the casino. Mrs. Scarvetti had just left to go shopping, and as she walked off, Big Frank had remarked that "There goes the woman who brought the bolt down on me."

Curious, Val had made bold to ask what Big Frank meant by that.

"In Italy they believe that when a man and a woman are meant for each other, when they first meet it brings down the lightning bolt of amore. It's like you are jolted to your core. You know, deep down, that she's the only one for you."

Now, sitting there staring into Misty's beautiful eyes, Val realized the Italian belief was true. He snapped his fingers and brought the eager beaver waiter over so they could order. As the waiter scooted off, Misty tilted her head and opened her mouth but hesitated.

"What?" Val asked. "From now on there will be no secrets between us."

"I need to know something important."

"Say it."

"Do you plan to be a wiseguy forever?"

There it was, out in the open. Val suspected that his future rested on his answer. "I've never had any plans one way or the other," he admitted. "I live day by day, taking what comes. But I can tell you this. It's easier to become a wiseguy than to stop being one. They don't like it when someone wants to quit. You learn too much, know too many secrets, where too many bodies are buried. Too many things that can put them in the slammer. So they take steps."

"What kind of steps? What would they do if you tell them that you don't want to be a wiseguy anymore?"

"They'll kill me."

"Just like that?"

"Just like that."

"But I thought Big Frank likes you. He saved you from the gutter. He put you to work with his own son."

"He did, he did," Val said. "But they don't think like you do, like normal people do. Big Frank did me a favor but for him it was business. That's how they divide up their world, into business and personal."

"I don't understand," Misty admitted.

"Here's how it works. You can, say, hate someone, and that's personal, but you don't whack him because he helps you make money, and that's good business. As much as Big Frank likes me personally, if I bail on him, he'll have me whacked because it's the smart business thing to do. See?"

No, Misty didn't. She was terribly confused. It sounded to her like they were fooling themselves. They pretended they could separate their personal feelings from their business dealings when the two were intertwined. "There's no way out? You can't sit down and reason with him?"

Val shook his head. "When a wiseguy says he wants to reason with you, it means he wants you six feet under."

"So you're stuck being a gangster until the day you die?"

"Not if you don't want me to be," Val heard himself say, and was astonished.

Misty picked up her glass of water. She hadn't counted on him coming right out with it like that. He was leaving it up to her. What she said next could change his life---and hers. Taking a sip, she peered at him over the rim. "Let's say I don't want you to be a wiseguy. How would you stop?"

"It's enough that you'd want me to," Val said. "I'd work out how."

"There might be a way?"

"It wouldn't be easy. They won't stop hunting for me as long as they think I'm alive. I'd have to disappear. To vanish off the face of the earth."

"How does someone do that?"

"There are ways. I could fake my own death. But I can't slip up. Any mistakes, however small, and they'd catch on." Val considered his other options. "Or I could go into hiding. Get as far from Vegas and Big Frank as I can. Go somewhere he's not likely to look." Suddenly Val realized what he was saying. Being on the run was bad enough. He couldn't ask her to go on the lam with him. What kind of life would that be?

Their food came and they ate in thoughtful silence.

Misty had a lot to ponder. Foremost was how she felt about the man across from her. She liked him. She cared for him. How much, though? He was looking for some sort of commitment based on what? One meal together? On knowing him less than twelve hours?

That was her mind speaking. When she tapped into her heart, her emotions were a flood tide. Her heart bid her to throw her arms around him and smother him with kisses. It made her feel warm all over, and not a little giddy.

What it boiled down to, Misty decided, was which she trusted more, her heart or her head? In the past she'd always relied on common sense to guide her. Emotions led people astray. Common sense rarely did.

They finished eating, and she still hadn't made up her mind.

Val consulted his watch. It was early yet. "What next?"

"For dessert? No thanks. I'm stuffed."

"No, after we leave here. Would you like to go dancing? Or maybe catch a movie?" Val hefted the bottle of wine. It was half-full. "We'll take this with us, have a good time."

Misty checked her own watch. "I should be heading home. Usually I turn in around ten on work nights."

"Why so early?" Val was lucky if he was under the covers by five a.m. on those rare nights when he was alone.

"I need my beauty sleep."

"If you never slept another wink, you'd still be the most beautiful woman in this town or any other."

Misty looked away.

"Can't you make an exception?" Val requested. "Just this once? For me? You pick it and we'll do it. Anything you want."

'No' was on the tip of Misty's tongue. Instead, she said, "You might think it silly but if you want to come along, I'll show you a special place I like."

Val crooked a finger, and the waiter was there to take his money. On their way out the maitre de invited them to come again soon. As the doorman opened the door for them, Val looped his arm with hers.

A breeze caressed them. Val brushed a stray strand of hair from her face and signaled the valet. "Where are you taking me, fair maiden?"

"You'll see."

"A mystery," Val grinned.

The valet wheeled the Neon to a stop and slid out. Val opened the door for Misty and she slid behind the wheel. Hurrying around, he climbed in. He was so happy to be with her, he could bust. For once in his life all was right with the world. He just hoped nothing spoiled it.

CHAPTER TWENTY-FOUR

The founder of Yuba City left an enduring legacy. In addition to the thriving urban center, there were, in no particular order, the Yuba River, Yuba Lake, Yuba Flats, Yuba Butte, Yuba Springs, Yuba Point, Yuba Gorge, and the distant Yuba Mountains. All named after Horatio Mortimer Yuba. As the first white man to visit that part of Nevada, he'd felt he had the right to name every landmark after himself. The Paiutes didn't mind. They thought he was touched in the head.

When it came time to decide where to build the town he envisioned, Horatio was torn between a belt of green along the Yuba River and another belt of green around Yuba Lake. He chose the former because it was closer to the main trail leading east and west.

Yuba Lake became a popular recreation area. Situated northwest of Yuba City, it drew boaters and fishermen and families that needed a break from the daily grind. At night it drew lovers who parked along the tree-lined gravel roads that meandered through the pristine wilderness.

Val had his first view of the lake when the Neon crested a hill. The full moon was mirrored in all it's magnificent lunar glory on the lake's shimmering surface. Well out from shore was the silhouette of a small island.

"Everyone calls it Lover's Island," Misty revealed when he mentioned it. She didn't tell him that she'd once rowed out there in a canoe with Jesse Stillwell, or that they'd almost done something she would have regretted.

"Even in the sticks people like their whoopie, huh?"

Misty downshifted as she neared the turnoff. She was preoccupied with the ebb and flow of her feelings, with desires she was finding it hard to keep in check. She almost had second thoughts about bringing him. Almost.

Val chuckled as they passed parked vehicle after parked vehicle. From the open rear window of one jutted a woman's naked foot, moving up and down. In a sports car a match flared, revealing unclothed breasts. "Small town or big city, people are the same everywhere." He glanced at Misty, wondering what her purpose was in bringing him here. It couldn't possibly be what it appeared to be. Not her. She was different. She was special. She was a virgin.

Misty wound deeper into the park, past the last of the lovers and on around to the north side of the lake where no one ever went because there were few trees and little cover. She braked close to the lake and switched off the engine. In the silence she swore she could hear her heart hammering.

"This is your special spot?"

"We have to walk to it. It's not far."

Except for a few headlights in the distance, the night was a black curtain.

"I hope you pack a gun when you're out here," Val said. "You could get mugged, or worse. Aren't there bears and stuff?"

Misty grinned. "The early settlers killed off the bears a long time ago. And there are hardly ever any muggings in Yuba City."

Val found that hard to believe. In the part of Chicago

where he grew up, a dozen muggings a night was average.

Opening her door, Misty slid out. She left her purse on the floor and her window down. Walking around to the passenger side, she held out her hand. "Come on."

Val had misgivings about traipsing around in the dark. Maybe there weren't bears but what about wolves and those big cats? He didn't ask for fear of coming across as a jerk. Thank God he was heeled.

Hand-in-hand they strolled to the water's edge. Small waves lapped in a soft rhythm.

Misty inhaled deep of the warm night air. The mirrored moon gave the illusion of being so close she could touch it. "Isn't it glorious? It makes you feel alive, makes you thankful for all the blessings the Lord bestows on us."

Val's mind wasn't on blessings at the moment. It was on her more than ample chest, on her slender waist, on the way her dress clung to her long legs. Abruptly he tore his eyes away, ashamed of himself.

"I'd like to live next to a lake some day," Misty said. "I'd like to have a nice home and kids. Two, three, maybe more. And a dog and a horse. A husband with a nine-to-five job who's always home on weekends, always there when we need him. Do you appreciate what I'm saying?"

Yes, Val did. She was telling him she wanted a normal life, not the kind of life the wife of a wiseguy endured. She didn't want her husband gone for days on end. She didn't care to live in constant fear that the next phone call would be the one letting her know her husband was never coming back.

Misty moved along the shore.

Val stayed at her side. A loud splash twenty feet out

caused him to spin, his hand darting under his jacket. "What was that?"

"A fish, silly goose."

"Don't they sleep at night?"

Misty laughed. "Fish aren't like us. They're always jumping. After insects, or for the fun of it, I guess."

"I bet the wolves and the cougars like fish," Val did some fishing of his own.

"The last wolf was shot and skinned about nineteen hundred, I think it was. As for cougars, no one has seen one in these parts for fifty years or better." Misty studied him. "You sure do worry a lot. Do you always think someone or something is going to attack you?"

"Not always," Val said, but that wasn't entirely true, for after he thought about it, he realized he lived in constant anticipation of being whacked or arrested. Rival Families, the Feds, local heat, they were all out to get him.

Misty spotted a rock outcropping, and smiled. "There's my special spot." She came here often to sit and stare out over the lake. She'd never brought anyone else. Not her father, not her mother, and not Jesse Stillwell. It was her spot and hers alone. Until now.

The outcropping was in the shape of a horseshoe. Shoulder high, the open end faced the water. Inside, a blanket of grass as soft as a comforter covered the ground. It was as private as could be. As private, say, as a motel room.

"What do you think?" Misty asked.

"Nice," Val said, uncertain exactly what he was supposed to say. A ring of rocks and some grass. Big whoop.

Misty sat and tucked her legs to her chest. Wrapping

her arms around her knees, she watched the wavelets lick the shore. Usually when she came here she felt a deep sense of peace, a sense that she was safely tucked in the embrace of the Almighty. Not tonight. Tonight she didn't feel peaceful at all. Her throat was dry, and she had a peculiar ache in her loins. She was sweating, too, something she rarely did except when she jogged.

Val picked up a flat stone the size of a half-dollar and skipped it across the water. The quiet, the night, the fact no one else knew where he was, filled him with a feeling he only ever felt a few times in his life, a feeling of pure, blissful peace. Like that time when he was fourteen and he'd drifted into St. John's to get out of a snowstorm. He'd spent half an hour in a back pew, in awe of the vaulted ceiling and the stained-glass windows, feeling a strange peace with the world.

"I won't bite. You can sit by me if you want," Misty said, patting the grass next to her. She looked straight ahead when he did, shifting so their bodies weren't touching. Her palms were slick, her legs prickly, as if she had a heat rash. Yet the night air was cool.

Val's sense of well-being shattered. He'd never been alone with a virgin before. How should he act? What should he say? If she were any other woman, he'd throw an arm over her shoulders and make suggestive small talk until she was primed. But that wasn't what a guy should do with a virgin. She'd be offended.

Misty coughed. "I better call my folks in an hour or so or they'll be worried about me."

"Do you like living at home with your parents?"

"Why wouldn't I?"

"Most women I know are out on their own. They have

an apartment or share a condo."

Misty liked how he called her a woman and not a girl like Jesse Stillwell always did. So what if she was barely out of high school. In her eyes she was full grown and should be treated accordingly. "That's city life, I reckon. Around here people tend to stay at home longer. Jesse Stillwell lives with his folks."

The more Val learned about the competition, the more convinced he became he could take the guy with one arm tied behind his back. "Tell me something, beautiful. How many girls in your class got pregnant while they were in school?"

"What a strange thing to ask."

"Not really. I can't get over how Brady Bunch this town is. In Chicago the newspapers are always going on about what they call an epidemic of teen births. How twenty out of every hundred girls are knocked up before the twelfth grade. It got so, they put daycare centers in the schools so the girls could have their babies looked after while they're in class."

Misty tried to imagine what that must be like. To be sitting in history class talking about the American Revolution while down the hall your child played with building blocks. "No one should ever get pregnant until they're ready for the responsibility."

"I agree," Val said. He'd heard a lot of stories from showgirls and others about pregnancies they'd had to abort and kids they'd had to put up for adoption. It tore them apart.

All this talk about babies was upsetting Misty. The ache in her loins was stronger. The itching had spread. She glanced at Val, at the crook of his leg, at his hips, and had a thought that made her dig her fingernails into her palms. She tried to blame it on the wine but she knew better.

Val tried to avoid looking at her. Every time he did, he imagined what she'd look like without her dress. The image made him hot enough to burst into flame. She was a *Playboy* centerfold made real, a *Penthouse* model in the flesh. And yet she'd hardly ever been touched, her lips hardly ever kissed. The only hands that had touched her nether regions were her own.

That last dazzling insight tantalized him like nothing ever had. To think, she'd never experienced a man down there. Her mount of Venus had never been stroked, her rose petal had never been kissed. That last thought jarred him. Why, tasting her would be like tasting the sweetest honey. His mouth began to water.

"Can I ask you something?"

"Anything," Val said, an odd rasp to his voice.

"What if---." Misty paused. "What if you gave up being a wiseguy to be with someone you cared for. What would it be like?"

"I painted you a picture earlier," Val said. "Unless we can come up with a way to throw the Scarvetti Family off my scent, it would be hell. We'd be on the run forever. We'd never be able to put down roots. We could never have kids or a dog or that horse you want."

"Oh."

She appeared so sad, Val put an arm around her. "Cheer up. It's not as if anything will happen between us. I see that now."

"You do?"

What Valeninto saw was him pressing his mouth to hers. Shaking his head to clear it, he said, "What kind of guy do you take me for? To lay a life like that on someone? You're better off not getting involved with a character like me."

"I am?" Deep down Misty knew he was right. She should stand up and leave. She should drive him to KCOW or wherever, and head home. From then on, they should maintain a casual relationship at work. That was what she should do. What she did was snuggle a little closer as if she were cold, which she wasn't.

Val squirmed inside. The warmth of her body was terribly arousing. He tried not to think of it. His fingers were primly perched on her shoulder, not lower where he wanted them to be. He should suggest they leave. He should get her out of there before he did something that upset her. From then on, he should treat her as a gentleman treated a lady. That was what he should do. What he did was squeeze her shoulders and slide his arm a little lower.

Misty was comparing him to Jesse Stillwell. Jesse, who always smelled of hay or fertilizer while Val smelled of fine cologne. Jesse, who was awkward and bumbling while Val was suave and sophisticated. Jesse, who dated her for eight months before he dared to put an arm around her while Val did it as if it were the most natural thing in the world to do.

Val thought of the showgirls he'd dated and contrasted them with Misty. The showgirls, who smelled of exotic perfumes. Misty, who smelled like a field of clover. The showgirls, who were so knowing, so forward, who weren't the least bit shy about their bodies. Misty, who knew so little, who was shy and hesitant, and saving herself.

At the same instant each of them said:

"Misty---."

"Val---."

"Ladies first." Val impulsively grinned and pecked her on the tip of her nose.

"I think we should go."

"So do I."

"You do?"

"Yeah."

"Then let's do it."

"Sure."

"I'm ready when you are."

"I'm ready."

"Then why aren't you getting up?"

"Why aren't you?"

For Val, it was one of those critical moments in his life when he was convinced that what he did next would have a bearing on his whole future. If they left it would be the end of them. He didn't want that. He didn't want that at all.

For Misty, her heart was fluttering like a butterfly's wings. She was scared to stay and she was afraid to leave so she sat and waited for fate to decide.

"Oh hell," Val said. He kissed her again. On the lips. He meant it to be a short kiss. A farewell kiss. A kiss that signified whatever they'd briefly shared was over and they would get on with their lives. But when their mouths touched, something incredible happened. He felt the lightning bolt. He'd kissed hundreds of women but he'd never experienced a kiss like this. Her lips were soft beyond soft, delicious beyond delicious, arousing beyond all arousal. He lost himself in the exquisite sensation.

Misty was caught up in a whirlwind of conflicting desires. She yearned to taste of the Forbidden Fruit but she was terrified. Terrified she felt this way. Terrified of the consequences. Her tongue met his and swirled around and around, and her breath caught in her throat. She heard someone moan and realized it was her.

When, at long last, Val pulled back, his body was a nuclear reactor on the brink of overload. Every cell was in the red zone. A scarlet haze filled the world. Misty, the ring of rocks, the lake, all were enveloped by the haze. He looked at her and saw something in her eyes he couldn't describe. Fear? Regret? It suddenly hit him that she might despise him for what he had just done. "Sorry," he blurted. "I couldn't help myself."

He wasn't the only one who couldn't. Misty was making more comparisons. Between the timid, lips-tight and rigid kisses of Jesse Stillwell, and Val's passionate kiss. To a kiss that speared to the center of her being. A kiss that pierced her heart, opening it wide. From the rent poured waves of longing that fueled the burning sensation between her legs. Lord help her, she wanted more.

"We can go now if---."

Misty placed her hands on his cheeks and drew his mouth to hers, kissing him as if she were devouring him. Her body was adrift in bliss. Her breasts were ripe to burst.

Val felt light-headed. He slid a hand between their bodies and cupped a mound. Misty groaned. Her body trembled, and damned if his didn't, too. When he tweaked a nipple she arched against him. That was when the full wonder of it dawned. Her cherry lips, those lips so seldom kissed, were his for the kissing. Her ripe body, so seldom caressed, was his for the caressing. Her womanhood, which had never been taken---was it his for the taking?

Near delirious with ecstasy, Misty couldn't say how she

wound up on her back or how her dress hiked so high, or how it was that he was lathering her bosom. When his mouth traveled lower she didn't think much of it. When his tongue glided below her belly button, she was confused.

"Val? Val? What are you---?"

Val was there.

"Oh! Oh! No. Not that. It's not---. We shouldn't---." Misty writhed and grabbed his hair. "Ohhh. Val. Ahhh. Please. Not like this. Oh. Oh." Misty had to exert all her strength to pull his head up. He seemed dazed.

"What?"

"Please."

"We can't stop."

"Please, Val."

Please what?" Val blinked. She was crying.

"For my sake."

"What?"

"You know."

"What?"

"You know."

God help him, Val did know. He reached up and touched a tear trickling down her cheek and brought the finger to his mouth and licked the tear off. "It's all right."

"For my sake," Misty repeated.

Val had been wrong. Those other crucial moments in his life weren't anywhere near as crucial as this. This was the moment that would define the rest of his life. This was the decision that would determine his destiny.

"What will it be, Val?" Misty asked.

Val didn't answer.

"What will it be?"

CHAPTER TWENTY-FIVE

In a room on the second floor of *The Radison*, Eddy the Book was going over the change in ownership papers to be signed the next day when there was a knock on the door. A titter gave him a clue who it was but he called out, "Who is it?"

"Open the frigging door."

"Louis?" Eddy said with feigned innocence.

"Open up."

Eddy the Book took his time to aggravate him. Plastering a smile on his face, he undid the chain. "To what do I owe this dubious honor?"

Cry Baby had one arm behind his back. Further down the hall stood Switch and the Wolfman, looking tired and bored. "If dubious means what I frigging think it means, I should bust your kneecaps." He swayed as he entered, his breath reeking of alcohol.

"A figure of speech, nothing more," Eddy said.

"You don't mind me stopping by this late?"

"Not at all," Eddy lied.

Cry Baby grunted and regarded the documents. "What are you doing?"

"I'm going over the paperwork. I want everything in order so I can be on my way back to Vegas by noon." The sooner Eddy was out of there, the happier he'd be.

"What can go wrong?" Cry Baby said. "I have everything under control. Go back and tell my pop that soon I'll be king of this frigging hick heap."

"Just so you keep a low profile, as he advised."

"Are you telling me what to do, Moses?"

Eddy bristled. "What did you just call me?"

"Moses. Isn't he the patri-something of your people?"

"The patriarch," Eddy said. "But how dare you?"

Cry Baby laughed. "Jesus. Don't get bent out of shape. I'm trying to do the right thing here I brought a peace offering to show you that you and me should be buds."

"I know better, Louis," Eddy said.

"You don't know squat." Cry Baby brought a plastic bag from behind his back. "Here. Take a look at these movies I got you at Video Mart. It's my way of saying thanks for all the trouble you've gone to. I'd have brought you a broad but I cruised the frigging streets for a frigging hour and couldn't find a single frigging hooker."

Eddy examined the movies and was surprised. One was *The Ten Commandments* starring Charlton Heston. The second was *Fiddler On The Roof*. Last was *Schindler's LIst*. He figured it was Lou's warped way of doing something nice. "I thank you," he said.

"Hey, no thanks necessary," Cry Baby said, slurring his words. "These are the kind of flicks your kind like, right?"

"They're some of my favorites," Eddy admitted.

"I thought so. I mean, that last one, I heard it was all about what happened to your people in World War Two, when the frigging Germans were gassing them and shit. Hell, there might even be some of your relatives in the movie. Wouldn't that be a kick in the pants? Seeing one of your---what do you call 'em?---ancestors being gassed?"

Eddy the Book wasn't a violent man but he came close to punching Lou Scarvetti in the face. He didn't mention that he'd already watched the movie twice, or how deeply it affected him.

"Are we golden?" Cry Baby asked.

"You've impressed me," Eddy said. He didn't say how.

Cry Baby beamed. "My second good deed of the night. I'm a regular Mother Theresa." He turned and shambled away, waving a hand in parting.

Quickly, afraid he couldn't control his temper much longer, Eddy shut the door. He heard Cry Baby laugh.

As if in a daze, Eddy walked to the nightstand. His hands were shaking. He stared at the phone, then snatched up the receiver and dialed the information operator for New York City. He gave the name of an olive oil company that dabbled in more than olive oil.

A voice that would scare small children answered on the third ring.

"Give me someone higher up," Eddy got right to it. "I have an important message the head of your Family will want to hear."

There was a pause. "Who is this?"

"Nevermind."

"You can tell me whatever you have to tell him."

"Don't play games," Eddy said. "I won't stay on the line long. Either pass me on or I'll hang up."

"If this isn't as important as you say---," the man began.

"It is. Tell him it's about Victor Scola."

A muffled exchange at the other end resulted in the man saying, "All right. Hold on. It might take a couple of minutes."

Eddy only had to wait half that long.

"What is this about an important message?"

"Victor Scola," Eddy said again.

"So I was told. The name is familiar. I'm listening."

"I understand that you and your associates are very interested in the whereabouts of a certain party." Eddy was deliberately vague in case the Feds or the cops had the line tapped.

"I'm still listening."

"Two words will suffice."

"What do you want for these words?"

"Nothing."

"You don't want money? What then? Name it, and if it's within reason, it's yours."

"I want nothing," Eddy repeated.

"Then why?" the man asked suspiciously. "No one does a thing like this for nothing. There has to be a reason."

"The reason is mine. You wouldn't understand."

"Let me hear the words, then."

"Yuba City."

Eddy the Book hung up. His hands were shaking worse and he'd broken out in a sweat. Sitting on the bed, he buried his face in his hands.

"God help me. What have I done?"

CHAPTER TWENTY-SIX

The day started off fine.

Cry Baby made it a point to sit in on the meeting with Arty Johnson's lawyer, Skimmer Hamilton, a wimp of a legal beagle more Chihuahua than Doberman. It went without a hitch. Eddy the Book and his father's own legal hounds knew their stuff. Arty Johnson nursed a flask the whole while and mumbled when asked questions. Cry Baby came close to slapping him to get his attention. The loser was well on his way to becoming a Grade-A lush.

After the meet, Eddy the Book and the lawyers split for Las Vegas. Cry Baby was puzzled when Eddy the Book came up to him, smiling, and shook his hand in parting as if they were good friends. He knew Eddy ranked him up there with bad breath and flat tires. Cry Baby couldn't figure Eddy's angle. But the important thing was that the accountant and the legal beagles were out of his hair.

Cry Baby could really cut loose.

He had another meeting coming up but he wasn't thinking about that. He was mulling the thing that had put a crimp in his great day. Valentino hadn't shown up yet. There hadn't been any sign of him since they saw him and the blonde sugartits coming out of *The Radison.*

It was unbelievable.

For one of Cry Baby's crew to mock his authority made him mad enough to punch a wall. When loverboy finally dragged his sorry ass back, Cry Baby was going to come down on him like a hammer on a human skull. He was talking splat city. The wiseguys in his crew must be taught that when they broke his rules, they paid the piper, mondo bigtime.

As if that weren't enough to frost Cry Baby, Val and the bimbo must be shacking up somewhere because she hadn't shown up, either. Cry Baby even got a call from her mother. Clarissa Lane apologized for bothering him, then went on---and on----about how her precious daughter hadn't come home last night, and how Misty never, ever, did anything like that because Misty wasn't one of *those* kind of girls, and would Mr. Scarvetti happen to know where she was? Cry Baby almost replied, "Yeah, one of my boys is off humping her brains out." But he was polite and said he had no idea, and wasn't it a shame the things young people did these days? Cry Baby thought that last was a good touch.

The mother had wondered if maybe she should call the cops. Cry Baby convinced her to wait a while. "Give your brat another day," he'd suggested. "I bet she'll drag her hot tamale tail home by then."

"Mr. Scarvetti, the way you talk," the mother said. "My Misty isn't a hot tamale or any other food. She's as decent a young woman as you'll find anywhere. And please don't mention tails."

"Why not? Every babe has one. Including you."

"Honestly, Mr. Scarvetti."

Annoyed, Cry Baby had said, "Your hubby must think you have a tail or we wouldn't be having this talk. Get me?"

"Are you saying what I think you're saying?"

"Go look at your butt in the mirror, lady, and you'll see what I mean." On that friendly note Cry Baby had hung up.

Now, a knock on the door intruded on Cry Baby's funk. "What is it?" he gruffly demanded.

The Wolfman poked his hairy head in. "That Todd guy is here to see you."

"The Program Director? Send him in."

Larry Todd entered. He was nervous as hell. He wanted to impress his new boss but he had no idea how to go about it. So much was going on, Larry couldn't make sense of it. Last night the chief engineer confided that he was involved in some sort of secret project, and then that morning two of the men in black went out to pound the streets with the sales staff, and when Sam and Billy came back a short while ago, they were pale and slick with sweat and wouldn't say why.

Larry took a seat and placed the clipboard and binder he'd brought in his lap. "Let me say right off the bat that I'm glad you've taken over, Mr. Scarvetti. A change in management might well lay the foundation for a new era here at K-COW."

Cry Baby laughed. "Cut the frigging bullshit, lame-o. Sucking up to me won't win you any points."

"Sir?"

"Let's get to it. From here on out we're not going to be named after a frigging cow. Starting as soon as you leave this office, we'll have new---," Cry Baby paused. "What do you call them again? Oh, yeah. Call letters.

"We will?" Larry said in confusion. "The FCC has given their permission for us to change?"

"Why does everybody keep bringing them up? You just do what I tell you. Let the DJ's know that from now on we're K-L-A S. KLAS." Cry Baby leaned back, smiling.

"What do you think? I picked my own initials. Louis Alphonse Scarvetti. It rhymes with class."

Larry wondered if he should point out that KLAS also rhymed with a certain part of the human anatomy. He decided he should keep quiet. "Great idea, sir."

"The first of many." Cry Baby fished in a jacket pocket and produced a folded sheet of paper. "I was up until four this morning making notes. Your department is the songs, right?"

"By and large. I want to point out, in case no one has mentioned it to you already, that we hired one of the most prestigious consulting firms in the country before we chose our current format. Creative Decisions, Incorporated, conducted a saturation survey and confirmed Country was the most viable. I have the results right here." Larry tapped the binder.

"Let me get this straight. You ding-a-lings forked over major green to some out-of-town yo-yo's who told you that wallowing in cow patties was the way to go?"

Larry squirmed in his chair. "Yes, sir, that's basically what we did, yes. It was Arty Johnson's idea."

"Stupid is as stupid does," Cry Baby said. "Now listen up. I've been giving it a lot of thought and I know how to make our station tops in Yuba City."

"You do?"

Cry Baby was pleased at how brilliantly he'd worked the plan out and couldn't wait to share it. "We're in the music business, right? We play music for people to listen to. Follow me so far?"

"I think so," Larry said.

"And the number one station is the one with the most listeners. Am I still right?"

"Yes, sir, absolutely."

"Well, since no two jerks like the same songs, the key to being number one should be frigging obvious. We'll go ice cream on their ass."

Larry wondered if his ears were working. "Ice cream, sir?"

"Yeah. Like Baskin-Robbins, that ice cream place. Ever been to one?"

"Yes, sir. I'd imagine everyone has."

"And how many flavors do they have? Just chocolate and vanilla?"

Larry was desperately trying to figure out what that had to do with their music. "No, sir. Last I heard, they have dozens of flavors."

"A gazillion of them," Cry Baby said. "And why? Because no two people like the same frigging flavor. So Baskin and that other guy give the dopes what they want. Every frigging flavor under the frigging sun. It works, too, doesn't it? They're the place everybody thinks of when they think of ice cream. Am I right again?"

Larry played it safe and said, "Baskin-Robbins knows ice cream, sir."

Cry Baby beamed. "What works for those two guys will works for us. We're going to have a Baskin-Robbins, what do you call it? Format."

"Sir?"

"Are you stupid or something?" Cry Baby thought he'd explained it perfectly. "Instead of a gazillion flavors we'll play a gazillion songs. All different kinds for all different people. That way, more of them will listen to us, and the more that do, the better our ratings will be. See how easy this works?"

"Oh. You mean we'll widen our audience base by playing a greater selection?"

"Bingo."

Larry thought he understood. "So you want me to work up a list of new songs? Retain a Country base but blend in Adult Contemporary or light Pop?"

"What the hell do Pepsi and Coke have to do with this, dipwad? Are you paying frigging attention? Hickweed music is out. Oh, we might play a cow song now and then for the hillbillies, but not that often." Cry Baby unfolded his sheet. "I've made a list of the stuff I want us to start airing. If we don't have what I want, go to a music store or K-Mart or someplace."

Unclipping a pen, Larry prepared to write. The new boss's idea was on the bizarre side but it might work if the music mix was carefully coordinated.

"For starters, I want four or five Frankie Valli songs an hour. Either his own stuff or what he did with the Four Seasons. You know. The classics. Oh What A Night. Rag Doll. Working My Way Back To You."

"Four or five an *hour*?"

"Yeah. I also want some of the old-timers thrown in. Dino, for sure. No one can croon like him. And old Blue Eyes, too. He's big with the retired fuddies."

"Dean Martin and Frank Sinatra?"

"Why do you repeat every frigging thing I say?" Cry Baby made a mental note to find out if a Program Director was essential. This one seemed a bit dense. "Where was I? We have the classics covered for the old geezers. Now we want something for the younger crowd. I was thinking Debby Boone. I know it's been a while but I really liked the one hit she had. And then we'll play some Beatles for the foreigners. Oh, and Elvis. We can't go wrong with the King."

"Debby Boone for the younger crowd?"

"You're doing it again, asswipe. What's wrong with her? I'm telling you here and now that we're not going to play any of that hard rock crapola. None of those sluts or boneheads you see on MTV. And no Madonna. Anyone who takes Jesus's mom's name in vain should be crucified."

Larry had an impulse to pinch himself to see if maybe he was still in bed and dreaming. "No sluts. No boneheads. And no Madonna. Got it."

"I'm not done. I've got a whole page here. We want to cover all the bases so we'll play some K. what's-her-face for the ballet tights set."

"The tight who?"

"I swear. You frigging repeat what I frigging say one more frigging time and I'll frigging kick your frigging teeth in. Got me?"

Larry swallowed. "Yes, sir. Got you."

"Good. Even a hickburg like Yuba City has to have six or seven of the ballet set. Guy tights. Girl tights. It makes no nevermind. We want them to listen, too." Cry Baby scanned his list. "For the blacks we'll throw in a little Michael Jackson although I heard he's not as dark as he used to be. They still like his music."

"Any particular songs of his, sir?"

"The ones where he grabbed his crotch. Those were the ones everybody seemed to like best."

"But this is radio, sir?"

"What's your goddamn point?"

"Nothing, sir."

Cry Baby checked his list. "I was listening to all kinds

of stations last night and I noticed how some have whole hours where they play just one kind of music. We'll do the same. Polka music, banjo music, Big Band music. And soundtrack music, too."

"Soundtrack music?"

Cry Baby glared.

"Sorry, sir."

"Cool movie music. None of that frigging The Sound of Music crap. I'm talking the Bond themes and music from The Magnificent Seven and that shark flick."

"Got it, sir."

"Good. There was one other type I liked. I heard it last night for the first time." Cry Baby ran a finger down the sheet. "Here it is. Gregorian Chant music. People like monks and nuns. It'll draw the church crowd."

"It will?" Larry quickly caught himself. "I mean, no doubt, sir."

Cry Baby held out the sheet. "Here's the list. All you have to do is break it down. Can you handle that?"

"No problem, sir," Larry said. He was thinking that if he typed real fast, he could have resumes in the mail by the end of the day.

"Good. Get cracking. Do this right and there's an extra hundred in your next paycheck. Screw up and you'll find out I wasn't joking about your frigging teeth."

Larry Todd got out of there.

CHAPTER TWENTY-SEVEN

The KCOW sales personnel, Billy Holliday and Sam Dowd, walked into Yuba City Hardware, one of their best clients. Ted Wilson, the fiftyish owner, always bought a modest amount of commercials.

Wiping his hands on his apron, Ted came around the counter to greet them. "Howdy, boys. How are things with you?"

Sam Dowd cleared his throat. "We're here to renew, Mr. Wilson. Your last schedule called for ten spots in weekend drive and two on Sunday during the Lutheran Hour."

Ted Wilson nodded. "I know what I bought." He stared at the two men in dark suits who had come in with Billy and Sam.

Pretty Boy and Dill stood behind the two salesmen. They didn't say anything.

Sam Dowd glanced at them, and coughed. "Can we interest you in more, Mr. Wilson?"

"Not now, no," Ted said amiably.

"Are you sure?" Billy Holliday anxiously asked.

"You boys know I'm on a tight advertising budget," Ted said.

Pretty Boy shouldered between the salesmen. "We want you to buy twice as many as before."

"I beg your pardon?" Ted said.

"Twenty commercials in drive time," Pretty Boy said,

"and four on Sunday."

"You must be joking."

"Twice as many, at triple what you paid before."

Ted Wilson wagged a finger under Pretty Boy's nose. "Are you insane? Why would I possibly do such a thing? And who do you think you are, anyway, coming into my store and telling me how much advertising to buy?"

By then Dill had slipped around behind him. Grabbing Wilson by the wrists, he twisted, and Wilson cried out.

Sam Dowd took a step toward them but stopped.

"Be reasonable, Wilson." Pretty Boy recited what Cry Baby had told him to say. "You're getting quality air time on the top station in town. Or it soon will be. And as a preferred customer, you have our guarantee that salesmen from the others stations won't come around bothering you, wanting you to advertise with them. If they do, give us a call and we'll see that they never come around again."

Ted Wilson was so livid, the veins in his neck bulged. "This is an outrage. It's extortion. I won't stand for it. As soon as you leave I'm calling the police."

"Think again," Pretty Boy said, and punched him. He landed three blows low down, but not too hard since Wilson was an old guy. When Wilson doubled over, gurgling, Pretty Boy pinched an earlobe. "We know where you live. The boys here tell us you have a wife and a nice home. And six grandkids. It would be a shame for anything to happen to them."

"Happen?" Ted Wilson gasped.

"You know. Your wife falls down the stairs. Or your house catches fire. Or one of the grandkids is the victim of a hit and run." Pretty Boy patted a bald spot on Wilson's dome. "It's up to you. What do you say? Do we have a deal?"

Ted Wilson sagged. "This can't be happening."

Pretty Boy kicked him in the knee.

It was a while before Wilson stopped thrashing and sputtering and could talk.

"I didn't hear you," Pretty Boy said. "What was your answer?"

"We have a deal," Wilson said, tears in his eyes.

Pretty Boy nodded at Dill, who let go. "Remember now. Not a word to anyone. This is just between us. If we hear you've been talking behind our backs, you won't like what happens." To Billy Holliday he said, "Write up the order and have him sign it. We'll be outside." He and Dill walked out.

Sam Dowd went to put a hand on Ted Wilson's shoulder but the owner slapped it away.

"Don't touch me. You stood there and did nothing."

"They told us if we interfered, they'd break our arms."

"Dear God. What have you gotten mixed up in?" Ted Wilson glanced at the front door, saw Pretty Boy staring in at them, and turned away. "Don't tell me. I don't want to know. Give me the contract so I can sign it and then get out of my store."

"I'm sorry, Mr. Wilson. I truly am."

"Go to hell. And take those vile thugs with you."

CHAPTER TWENTY-EIGHT

Switch woke Cry Baby from a nap at four in the afternoon. Cry Baby sat up, glared at the sofa, and growled, "They call this thing comfortable? I want a new frigging couch in here tomorrow. I'm a frigging executive now. I should have the frigging perks that go with it."

"Will do, Mr. Scarvetti."

Cry Baby swung his feet to the floor. "Wolfman, some java, heavy on the sugar. I have to get my blood flowing." He stretched and rose and moved to his desk. "One of you turn the speakers on. I want to see if that brain-dead Program Director did as I told him."

From the large speakers mounted in opposite corners of the ceiling blared the final notes of *Walk Like A Man*. "And that was Frankie Valli and the Four Seasons on the all-new K-L-A-S, the station with class. This is Susie Q bringing you the best of the best. Before Frankie we heard the Rejects, a cut from their latest CD, Polish Polka A La Carte. Before that it was the Ski Chase from the James Bond movie, On Her Majesty's Secret Service. After a break from our sponsors, I'll be back with You Light Up My Life by Debby Boone."

"Turn it off," Cry Baby said, his brow creasing. It sounded okay but something was a little off. He couldn't pin it down. "What do you guys think? Not bad, huh?"

"Gets my vote," Switch said.

The Wolfman was pouring coffee. "I'd sure listen to it,

Mr. Scarvetti," he said. But only if it were the last radio station on earth and someone was holding a gun to his head.

Cry Baby snapped his fingers. "I've got it!" Pressing the intercom, he barked, "Todd. Get your ass in here."

Larry Todd was printing a resume. He planned to send it to a small station in Alaska. Until two days ago he'd dreamed of moving up in the world, of becoming PD at a top station in a major market. Now he didn't care where he worked so long as he got out of there. Jumping up, he hurried down the hall, and at his knock, was admitted by the guy with the short blond hair. "Yes, sir, Mr. Scarvetti?"

"I just gave a listen," Cry Baby said. "You've done good but there's one more improvement we need to make. It's the damn disc jockeys."

"You want some of them replaced?"

"There's a thought but not yet. No, I'm talking about how they talk. Give a listen to hippo. She sounds like she was born in the backwoods. Go tell her to lose the twang. Have all of them talk like, oh, I don't know, like they're from New Jersey or someplace where there's culture and shit. If they don't know how to do it, have them pinch their noses."

"Do what now, sir?"

"Here. Give a listen." Cry Baby pinched his own nose. "Notice the difference when I talk? It makes a whole new sound."

Larry looked up, hoping the ceiling would fall on him. No such luck. "I'll get right on it, sir. No more backwoods. Pinch their noses." He departed in a rush.

Cry Baby let go of his nose. "Could be I was wrong about that pusscrumb. He's a go-getter."

The Wolfman brought over a mug of steaming coffee. "What's on tap next, Mr. Scarvetti? Any more meetings you have to take?"

"No. The bimbo was supposed to set me up with the mayor but she's been gone all frigging day. Which reminds me. Any word from Valentino yet?"

Switch and the Wolfman shook their heads.

"There must be something wrong, boss," Switch said. "Val would never leave us in the lurch like this."

"Says you," Cry Baby said. "What could it be besides the babe? It's not as if he's been whacked. No one who would want to snuff him knows where we are."

"Maybe you should give your father a call, Mr. Scarvetti," the Wolfman suggested.

"Like hell. Anyone does, I'll shoot them. This is my show, mine and mine along. Any problems, I deal with it. Any hassles, I smooth them over. I'm going to prove to him once and for all that I've got what it takes to run the Family." Cry Baby turned to the wall clock. "The others should be back in an hour or so and we'll go grab a bite to eat. Then everyone is to rest until later. I want you bright-eyed and bushy-tailed so we don't have any frigging screw-ups tonight."

"There won't be, Mr. Scarvetti," Switch said.

Cry Baby gazed out the open door at the reception area and the empty front desk. Where in hell could Val and the bimbo be? he wondered.

CHAPTER TWENTY-NINE

"I want to call my mother."

"You can't."

Misty Lane bit her bottom lip. The stark scenery flashing past her Neon matched the stark ache in her heart. "They care for me, Val. It's not right, my not letting them know. They'll worry themselves to death. My mom will cry herself sick."

"We've been all through this, "Val said. A twinge of guilt nipped at him but he refused to change his mind, not when their lives were at stake. "You can call them when we're sure we're safe, not before." He glanced at her and was alarmed at how tired she looked, and how sad. This was supposed to be the greatest day of her life and she was miserable. He took a hand off the steering wheel to stroke her cheek. "I know this is rough on you. I know it's rough on them. But it's for their own good. If Cry Baby suspects they have any idea where we are, he'll have their fingers and toes chopped off one-by-one until they tell him."

"He would do that?"

"He would do that."

"What kind of monster is he?" Misty asked, appalled.

"The worst there is. The human kind." Val yawned. They hadn't had any sleep in more than a day and a half now, and it was taking a toll. He'd give anything for six to eight hours of undisturbed slumber. "Are you getting cold feet?"

"Do you really think I would?" Misty countered. She would stand by her decision until death did them part. It was bold of her, she knew. It was mad, it was impetuous, it was foolish. But she had no regrets. He'd asked her and she'd said yes and soon she would be his and he would be hers.

Val scanned the horizon for the Las Vegas skyline. He had stuck to secondary roads as a precaution and the trip was taking twice as long as it would if they took the interstate. That was okay, though. He dared not take chances with Mindy's life.

As if she could read his mind, she asked, "How will we know when it's completely safe for me to call them."

"I'll know," Val said.

"How safe is it for us to be going to Vegas?"

"They probably aren't hunting for us yet. It'll take them a few days to figure out I've skipped. We'll whisk into Sin City, grab the money, and split."

"I wish you wouldn't call it that."

"Sorry."

"What if you're wrong? What if they're waiting for you?"

Val had gone over the setup a dozen times. He did so again to soothe her. "I've never told anyone about my safe deposit box. No one will be at the bank. We should be in and out in under ten minutes. We'll drive to Reverend Goodfellow's Chapel of Heavenly Hereafters and say our 'I do's'. Then it's on to California. We can lose ourselves there."

"How much money is in your safe deposit box?"

"It could be ten grand. Maybe as much as twenty." Val seldom kept track. Like most wiseguys, money meant little to him. And like most of them, he kept a secret stash for emergencies.

Misty thought about her parents and blinked back tears. By eloping she had gone against everything her father and mother taught her. She'd violated their trust, their love. She looked at Val, at how handsome he was, and told herself he was worth it.

Val smiled but he was deeply conflicted. He regretted skipping out on Cry Baby, regretted even more failing in his duty to Big Frank. He had to remind himself that to them he was just another soldier. He'd miss the crew, though, miss Switch and Pretty Boy and the Wolfman and Dill. They were like brothers.

Switch he'd miss the most. They'd shared some fine times, the two of them, fun and danger in equal degrees. Switch would guess what he'd done but Switch wouldn't rat on him. More than likely, Switch would try to cover for his absence to delay Cry Baby's search. That was the kind of friend Switch was.

Not that Val was all that worried about Cry Baby. His real worry was the Family's chief enforcer. Sooner or later Big Frank was bound to sic the Iceman on him, and there was no escaping the Iceman. Word was, the Iceman could track anyone, anywhere, anytime. But even the Iceman needed a trail. A paper trail, credit cards, ATM use, motel registers, something.

Val wasn't going to leave one.

The next moment warms fingers entwined with his and Misty said softly, "I love you."

Val wasn't used to it yet. The words, the reality, were too new. He'd said it twice since he'd proposed and each time he'd had to force it out. For her sake, though, he forced it again. "I love you, too."

"Tell me everything will be all right and I'll believe you."

"Everything will be all right." Val couldn't look her in the eyes when he said it.

CHAPTER THIRTY

At ten-thirty that night Cry Baby took his travel kit into the bathroom. He was alone, for once. His crew had things to do. The only other person in the station was the DJ.

Whistling the tune to *I've Got You Under My Skin*, Cry Baby unzipped the kit. He brushed his teeth twice. He flossed. He gargled for three minutes. A liberal sprinkling of *Brut* on his neck and cheeks gave him the manly smell he liked. Next he applied 'greasy kid stuff', as he liked to call it, to his hair. Uncertain whether he looked better with the top button to his shirt undone, or the top two, he experimented and left the top three unbuttoned. He also left his jacket open so his guest could appreciate his studliness. He thought about stuffing a sock down below but decided not to. That might be overdoing it.

Cry Baby sat at his desk to impress her with his executive bearing. Then he got up. She wasn't coming for that kind of business. He sat on the sofa but didn't like being so low to the floor. It made him look shorter than he was. He walked over to the coffee maker, leaned against the wall, and adopted a cool expression.

It was important he impress her.

Cry Baby remembered how cool Al Pacino had been when putting the moves on Catwoman. He mimicked Pacino's body language. If Joe could do it---and Pacino was The Man---so could he.

His mouth posed a problem. He couldn't make up his mind whether he looked better smiling or scowling or whether he should just sort of have a neutral mouth. He stepped to the mirror and curled his lips all kinds of ways. He was still practicing when he heard a rustling sound behind him. He whirled, his hands going for his pistols. But it wasn't an enemy. It was her.

Meriam Johnson had been standing in the doorway for a couple of minutes not believing what she was seeing. Here was this Mobster, this tough guy who scared her husband pissless, preening and primping like some kid going to a prom. She would have laughed but after what her pathetic excuse for a soul mate had told her, she wasn't about to tick Louis Scarvetti off.

Arty had finally told her all of it.

Meriam had badgered him. She'd railed and ranted and pleaded and shed a few sham tears. In the end, though, her theatrics failed to pry the truth from him.

Vodka took the credit. Arty had been drinking steadily since he came back from Vegas, gulping it down like a fish gulped water. The only time she saw him without his flask was when he passed out and it fell from his hand.

Meriam refilled it and revived him. "Why I'm so nice to you, I'll never know," she raked her verbal claws.

"You've stood by me through thick and thin over the years, haven't you?"Arty had said. His eyes were so bloodshot they'd looked like roadmaps done in red ink.

"And what thanks do I get?" Meriam retorted. "You won't even tell me how we lost our station."

To her surprise, Arty burst into tears and started babbling. Between sobs and swigs he spilled the details.

Meriam learned everything. She'd never considered him much of a man. She considered him even less of one now. Her hunch had been right. The Mafia had taken over. The fucking Mafai.

Arty acted as if it were the end of the world and maybe for him it was.

Meriam wasn't about to give up without a fight. She had too many years invested, too many nights where she'd faked getting off so her wimp of a man would feel like one.

Meriam was positive she could turn this disaster to her advantage. There had to be a way. The little guy, Scarvetti, liked her. He'd made that plain. How could she capitalize? How could she fan his interest? How could she hook a guy who probably had his pick of willing women? She was too pragmatic to kid herself. She wasn't young anymore. Her personal Battle of the Bulge had been lost long ago. To snare Scarvetti she couldn't rely on her looks.

It set her to thinking about her Oklahoma cowboy. How he was the best lover she'd ever had. Not because he was well hung or the world's best kisser. No, his appeal lay in how he liked to do anything and everything, especially the kinky stuff Arty regarded as yucky. And the kinkier the cowboy had been, the more she liked it.

Perhaps the same thing would work with Scarvetti, Meriam reasoned. She'd gone to her closet after a hot bath. At the back was her stash of underthings and sex toys. She'd selected a sheer Frederick's number with holes for her nipples and a cutaway crotch. Black nylons and garters and high-heels complemented her ensemble. She'd thrown an overcoat on, buttoned up, and here she was.

Smiling, Meriam sashayed into the office. Scarvetti stared at her strangely, she thought. "Here I am, handsome, right on time. Just like you wanted."

Cry Baby got as hard as the crowbar he'd used to whack Vic Scola. "Sweet Jesus."

"What's the matter?" Meriam asked, afraid things had gone to hell before they even started.

"You look just like her."

"Like who?"

Cry Baby wasn't about to let her know she looked like his mother. "It's not important. Close the door. We don't want anyone waltzing in on us."

No, they didn't, not with what Meriam planned.

Cry Baby moved to the desk and leaned back. Folding his arms and posing like he was in a movie, he said, "Here's how this works, bitch. You want answers about how I got this station? Make me happy and you'll get them. But I'm warning you in advance, I'm not easy to please."

Meriam decided not to tell him that she already knew. Seductively placing one foot in front of the other, she undid a button at a time on her overcoat. His throat bobbed when she reached for the last one. "Don't you worry, big man," she said. "I aim to please."

No one had ever called Cry Baby 'big' before. Wetting his lips, he said, "That chumpwad hubby of yours never said what a hot babe he has for a wife."

The final button came undone. Meriam slowly opened her coat and thought his eyes would pop from his head. From a coat pocket she drew fur-lined handcuffs and a whip.

"Hurt me," Cry Baby said.

CHAPTER THIRTY-ONE

Pretty Boy and Dill found it hard to believe the KWIN transmitter building wasn't guarded.

"Why would it be?" Howard Branigan said. "Most people are too afraid of being electrocuted to go anywhere near one." He added that for safety's sake, transmitters were located away from densely populated areas. Warning signs were usually enough to keep the curious and the stupid away.

KWIN's transmitter was northeast of Yuba City on a ten-acre plot the station leased from a rancher. The plot was fenced. The nearest house was the rancher's half a mile away.

Dill used wire cutters on the chain. The building was locked but Pretty Boy was good with a pick. Dill stood guard while the chief engineer fired up KWIN's backup transmitter.

"The trick will be whether their own engineer is listening," Howard said. "I called over there today to shoot the breeze. Lenny, his name is. He told me he's spending the night with his girlfriend. Hopefully, she'll keep him so busy, he won't have the radio on. Otherwise, he'll catch on right way and rush out here to see what's going on."

"Bad for him if he does," Pretty Boy said.

"What will you do?"

"No witnesses, Mr. Scarvetti said."

The ominous import hit Howard like a ton of

capacitors. "No one one said anything about hurting people. Promise me there won't be any violence."

"Why would I promise you something as stupid as that?" Pretty Boy said. He grinned a fierce grin. "Lenny shows up, Lenny is history."

Howard hadn't bargained on this. It was what he got for not saying no when the little lunatic told him how they were going to get their hands on a new transmitter. Make that a new used transmitter.

There was a metallic sound. Pretty Boy had a pistol in his hand and was ratcheting the slide to feed a round into the chamber.

Howard was stupefied. Even more so when the other one, the big one, turned from the door drawing a cannon from a shoulder holster. Howard wanted out. Stealing a transmitter was one thing. Murder another. But as he opened his mouth to say he'd changed his mind, Pretty Boy wagged his pistol.

"You've got a job to do. Get cracking."

Howard never worked so fast in his life. Once the backup was on-line, he shut down the main transmitter and disconnected it. Pretty Boy helped unfasten the bolts that held it to the concrete floor. Next, they broke the unit down into sections. Then the guy with the cannon wheeled the flatbed truck they'd rented up to the building and brought in a dolly so everything could be loaded. The pair covered the bed with a canvas and tied the canvas down, and they were ready to go.

Howard's clothes were soaked with sweat. He climbed into the cab, bowed his head, and closed his eyes. When they got to the KLAS transmitter site, he'd replace the KLAS main with the KWIN main.

Once he had his money, Howard vowed, the first chance that came along, he was taking off for parts unknown.

Beeping sounds brought his head up.

Pretty Boy was punching numbers into a Motorola mobile phone which had been clipped to his belt under his jacket. Big as a brick, they were hugely expensive. He put it to his ear. "We got it. No hitches. It's a go at your end."

"What's a go?" Howard asked.

"You don't want to know," Pretty Boy said.

Dill laughed.

CHAPTER THIRTY-TWO

Ten minutes after getting Pretty Boy's call, Switch and the Wolfman pulled up to the fence that surrounded the property where KDLR's transmitter stood. Switch used a hacksaw on a chain on the gate, and they were in.

KDLR had five towers. They hurried to the middle one, the Wolfman toting a gym bag.

"We better be careful," Switch said, pointing at a sign with large letters: WARNING. HIGH VOLTAGE.

"Don't touch anything and you'll be fine," the Wolfman said, craning his neck to see the blinking lights at the top.

"I saw an electrician who got fried once," Switch mentioned. "He looked like burnt bacon."

The Wolfman set the gym bag down. Opening it, he took out a flashlight and played the beam over the timers, detonators and plastique he'd brought.

Switch was scanning the area, a switchblade in his hand "I've been meaning to ask you. How come you got tabbed for explosives?"

The question swept the Wolfman back in time to the day Big Frank called him in and said four magic words.

"I need a favor."

"Anything, Mr. Scarvetti," the Wolfman had said. "You know that."

Big Frank shook his head. "Here me out, Richie. I'm not going to ask you to pick up a pizza. This is something important. Something you might not want to do."

"You took me in, gave me a job when no one else would. You've always treated me like a person, not a freak. I'd do anything for you, Mr. Scarvetti. Anything at all."

"Would you die for me?"

The Wolfman didn't' hesitate. "Sure."

"By die, I mean be blown to bits."

The Wolfman had puckered his eyebrows.

"A man in my position has to be prepared for every contingency, Richie. Which is why I like to have at least two soldiers who are good with explosives. Just in case, you understand?"

The Wolfman had nodded.

"Years ago I sent Lefty and Domino to a guy who knows all about blowing things up and he taught them the trade. But as you know, Lefty is getting on in years and his hands aren't as steady as they used to be. I need someone to take his place. Someone who isn't the nervous type. Someone like you."

Flattered, the Wolfman had said he'd be happy to do it.

"There will be an extra two hundred a month for you from now on but don't let the money sway you. It's risky work. Not quite as risky as the old days when they used dynamite and nitro. Now they use plastic explosive, C-4 and like that. It doesn't blow up when you breathe on it."

"I want to. Honest."

"Okay. But don't come back here missing an arm or a leg and say I wasn't level with you."

That was then. Now, the Wolfman bent over a timer. A twist of his wrist and it was set. He did the same with a second packet.

"Why blow just this one tower?" Switch asked. "Why not all of them?"

"No need," the Wolfman said. "Cry Baby did some checking. If only one of these babies goes down, the signal is for crap. KDLR will have to shut down until a new tower can be brought in. That could take months."

"That Cry Baby," Switch said. "As much as I hate to admit it, he thinks of everything."

The Wolfman stepped to the tower and attached the first packet. He did the same on the other side with the second. "We have thirty minutes to get clear."

"Plenty of time," Switch said. "We'll be back at the station when the fireworks go off. A perfect alibi."

"Wish I could see it," the Wolfman said. He'd grown to like the explosions, exactly as the man who taught him, a crusty codger known as Six-Fingered Joe, said he would.

They used to go to a Mob-owned quarry to practice. The first time he set off a charge, using an old-fashioned plunger, the Wolfman caught Six-Fingered Joe studying him. It was a small charge and the blast wasn't any great shakes but the Wolfman had been thrilled by the roar and the concussion and the display.

"Yeah, I was watching you," Joe replied when asked. "I can always tell who has it and who doesn't. The ones who don't will flinch or look away or cover their ears. They're nothing but wimps. I always tell them to take a hike." Joe had smiled. "Guys who act like you did, like a kid on the Fourth of July, are naturals for the job."

The Wolfman missed Six-Fingered Joe. They'd kept in touch until an accident separated his mentor from most of his major body parts. Word was, Joe had been working with nitro. It was nitro that took Joe's thumb and three fingers in the first place, and he liked to set some off now and then to show he wasn't afraid of the stuff. He should have left well enough alone.

"You taking a stroll or what?" Switch said from a dozen feet ahead.

The Wolfman caught up.

To the south was an isolated farmhouse, too far off for them to worry about being seen. Their car, yes, but they'd stolen it, and anyway, the farmer would think they were with KDLR.

Switch got behind the wheel. He gunned the motor and peeled out, dust spewing from under the rear tires. A dirt road brought them to a highway.

Traffic was light. They ditched the stolen Chevy in a motel parking lot, walked six blocks, and got a cab.

The Wolfman held the gym bag on his lap the whole way to KLAS.

The building was quiet. Midnight was sign-off and it was almost four a.m. Static crackled from the speaker over the receptionist's desk.

The Wolfman had just set the gym bag down when a strangled cry came from Cry Baby's office.

Switch had a switchblade out and open before the cry faded. He darted to the left of the door.

The Wolfman drew his piece and moved to the right of it. They looked at one another.

"Together on the count of three," Switch whispered. A louder screech galvanized him into gripping the doorknob. "To hell with it. You take low. I'll go high."

They burst in, Switch's arm cocked to throw, the Wolfman's finger around the trigger. Both abruptly stopped, their eyes widening.

Cry Baby was on his hands and knees, bucking up and down. His wrists were handcuffed and he had tape over his mouth. He was was naked as the day he was born. So was the women riding him as if he were a bronco and she were Calamity Jane. Smacking his backside with a whip, she thrust her hips in abandon.

"Mr. Scarvetti!"Switch exclaimed.

"Mr. Scarvetti?" the Wolfman echoed.

Cry Baby looked up. It seemed to take an effort for him to focus. He roared at them, the tape muffling his words. "Glef dog fluff old of heff, yeff fluffheffs."

Switch and the Wolfman backed out and Switch slammed the door.

"God in heaven."

"If that didn't strike me blind," the Wolfman said, "nothing will."

"We shouldn't stick around," Switch advised.

"I hear that." The Wolfman snagged his gym bag on the fly. "I can use a drink."

"Make mine a double," Switch said.

CHAPTER THIRTY-THREE

The Yuba City Chief of Police arrived at KLAS at eight a.m. sharp.

Chief Lester Poindexter looked around in puzzlement. There was no one at the front desk. He called out but no one answered. The door to the main office was open so he peered in. A leather whip lay in the middle of the floor. Scratching his Adam's-apple, Chief Poindexter walked down the hall to the control room. A glass partition let visitors watch the DJ's.

Hoss was on the air. He smiled and waved.

Chief Poindexter nodded and returned the gesture. His bewilderment grew when Hoss pinched his nose and spoke into the microphone.

"Those were the Brothers of St. Clemens and their new hit, Tempora Mutantur, Nos El Mutantur In Illis. Next up on the all-new K-L-A-S is the King, Elvis with Hound Dog. But first this traffic update brought to you by the fine folks at Yuba City Hardware."

Chief Poindexter saw the ON AIR light go off. He was about to go in when the door to the production room opened and out came Duke Banner, the John Wayne fan. Poindexter had met all the DJ's at one time or another at various functions and knew them by name. The last time he saw Dukie had been on Founder's Day at the KCOW booth. "Morning."

Duke hooked his thumbs in his leather belt and

ambled over as if he were eleven-feet-four-inches tall instead of the other way around. "Howdy, badge-toter. What brings you here?"

"I was hoping to speak to the new owner."

Duke scowled. "There's no tellin' when that jasper will show up. He doesn't exactly keep banker's hours."

"You don't sound happy about having him for your new boss," Chief Poindexter remarked.

"I ain't. That hombre insulted Susie Q. I ought to have stomped him into the ground but she wouldn't let me."

"What's with all the new music your station is playing these days?"

"It's the new boss's brainstorm," Duke said. "Comes from suckin' on too much loco weed, if you ask me." He clomped off in his cowboy boots.

Chief Poindexter did more Adam's-apple scratching. Lanky of build, with salt-and-pepper hair, he'd been in charge of the YCPD for going on fifteen years. He knew that to some folks he resembled a two-legged turkey vulture but under his deceptive frame lurked a keen-eyed hawk.

Poindexter took great pride in the town and the people who called it home. As well he should, given he was born and bred there.

A commotion at the entrance drew the Chief to the reception area. Based on the descriptions he'd been given, the new owner and four of his underlings had arrived. At the sight of them, the Chief felt a surge of anger.

Poindexter worked hard to keep Yuba City safe. Derelicts were persuaded to be derelict elsewhere. Ex-cons were discreetly given the choice of moving on or going back to prison. Those with gang links or rap sheets were advised that the climate wasn't conducive to their health. Put simply, wolves in any guise weren't welcome in Yuba City. Any who tried to shear the Chief's sheep regretted it.

Poindexter knew bad apples when he saw them, and the five men coming toward him might as well have trouble with a capital-T branded on their foreheads. The quintet in dark suits stopped and eyed him as he would a Hell's Angel. Forcing a smile, he offered his hand. "Mr. Scarvetti? What luck. I was under the impression you might not show up until later."

Cry Baby would rather be in bed. Thanks to Meriam, he had bruises where he'd never had bruises before. His legs, his backside, were so sore, he couldn't bear to sit. He'd come in early for a reason, namely, to find out if there was any flak from his crew's nocturnal activities. Apparently it was well he had. "Let me guess. The police chief, right?"

Poindexter introduced himself and they shook.

"Come into my office, "Cry baby said. "My associate, Mr. Vario, will get us some coffee. I don't know about you but I need something to get me going in the morning."

"I take mine black." Poindexter was thinking about that name, Scarvetti. When he'd first heard the mayor mention it, it rang a vague bell. Now he was sure he had run across it somewhere. He noticed that the associates, as Scarvetti called them, had spread out around the office.

"To what do I owe this honor?" Cry Baby asked, carefully easing into his chair.

"I reckon you haven't seen the morning paper yet," Chief Poindexter said. "All the years I've been on the force, the worst I've had to deal with was the time Ed Blake's wife stabbed him in the leg for fooling around with her sister. Then last night all hell broke loose around here. One of your competitors had their main transmitter stolen, the other had a tower destroyed, the man who used to own this station shot himself, a car was stolen and---."

Cry Baby straightened. "Wait a second. Back up. What was that about Arty Johnson?"

"He killed himself sometime around five to five-thirty this morning. His wife told us that she heard a noise, went downstairs to investigate, and there he was, dead on the floor."

Cry Baby recalled that Meriam had left the station about half past four. He wondered if that dope, Johnson, was up waiting for her. Had Meriam told Arty where she'd been and what she'd been up to? He could see it driving the weenie over the edge. Not that Cry Baby cared. He didn't need the lush anymore. "I'm sorry to hear that. I liked Mr. Johnson."

Chief Poindexter waited for him to ask about the other incidents. When he didn't, the Chief said, "Am I to take it you haven't heard about KWIN's main transmitter going missing, either? The owner tells me that no one has ever stolen a radio station transmitter before."

""Really?" Cry Baby had figured everybody did it, that stealing transmitters was as common as, say, hijacking trucks. "And that other station---what is it again? KDLR? They had a tower blown up?"

Chief Poindexter had said no such thing. He'd mentioned it was 'destroyed'. "That's why I'm here."

"It is?" For a moment Cry Baby worried he had somehow been linked to the crimes.

"Did anything happen to your station? If not, it would strike me as strange. I mean, the other two were hit but not yours?"

Cry Baby inwardly smiled. The lawman thought he was being clever. "Nothing has happened to the station, no. But we're worried about two of our employees."

"How so?"

"They're missing."

"Missing as in disappeared?"

Cry Baby nodded. "One is a member of my personal staff, Michael Corcione. The other is Misty something-or-other, our secretary." He never could remember the damn bimbo's last name.

Chief Poindexter stood. "Misty Lane? She's missing? Why wasn't my office notified?"

"They haven't been gone all that long," Cry Baby said. "I planned to call today."

The Chief touched his hat brim. "I'm sorry to cut this short, Mr. Scarvetti, but I'd better go talk to her parents. I know them well. They're nice people. He made for the door. "Lost and damaged property is one thing. A missing person is another. I'll get back to you as soon as I can."

"You do that. Nice meeting you."

The lawman departed.

"Want we should follow him and keep an eye on him, boss?"Dill asked.

"What for? He doesn't have anything on us." Cry Baby chuckled. "If that was the best law this hickville has to offer, we don't have a thing to worry about."

CHAPTER THIRTY-FOUR

Cry Baby had the world by the gonads and loved it. Everything was going his way. He could do no wrong. It was as if his fairy godmother had gotten off her lazy ass and was making things work in his favor. His luck was so good, he wished Yuba City had a casino so he could put it to the test.

As his limo cruised toward KLAS a week after his chat with Chief Lester Poindexter, Cry Baby cranked down a window, breathed deep of the cool morning air, and flashed his teeth at pedestrians.

He was top dog, just as he'd planned.

Yuba City was under his thumb.

His competition was dead in the water. According to the newspaper, KDLR would be off the air indefinitely due to some sort of delay in acquiring a new tower. KWIN was operating, but according to Howard Branigan, their backup transmitter reached less than half as many listeners as their main had.

KLAS, meanwhile, was purring like an electronic kitty. The new transmitter ran as slick as the edible body oil Meriam like to rub over him and lick off. Branigan had painted the exterior panels so the transmitter looked nothing like it did when it was KWIN's. Cry Baby suspected the guy did such a good job of disguising it because he was in a panic about the feds but he gave Branigan a bonus anyway.

KLAS had a new secretary, too. Cry Baby gave the job to Meriam. It was her idea. They were lying breast to cheek one night when she'd mentioned how lonely it was around her place with Arty gone and how she needed something to take her mind off the tragedy, and wouldn't it be great if she filled in for the blonde bimbo since she already knew all the ropes and could be near him during the day as well as at night?

Cry Baby hired her. He needed someone to answer the phone and make appointments anyway. Plus she was right there if he wanted a poke in the middle of the afternoon. All he had to do was call her in to take dictation.

Business executives sure knew how to live.

As for running the station, everything was roses. The announcers were toeing the line and not giving him any lip about the change in format. The midget, Duke, glared at him a lot but Cry Baby chalked that up to Duke being a Barnum and Bailey reject. Ordinarily, Cry Baby wouldn't let anyone get away with treating him as if he were armpit odor but it was nice to have someone around who was shorter than he was.

The DJ's had gotten the hang of the cultured accent, as Cry Baby liked to call it. Just yesterday he was walking past the control room and saw the sperm whale, Susie Q, pinch her nose and spout off about the great used cars at Slim's Vehicle Emporium.

A new work-and-news schedule was another of Cry Baby's brainstorms. He'd noticed how KWIN covered local news a lot more in-depth than KLAS. So he called in the announcers and told them that from now on each of them would spend two hours a day gathering news. The promise of an extra fifty a week in their pay envelopes nipped any squawking in the beak.

"I want us to be the place where everybody in town comes to for information," Cry Baby had wrapped up his spiel. "It's not enough that we beat the pants off the other radio stations. I want to beat the newspaper, too."

To that end, since the paper reported car accidents, KLAS started airing them, too, on a segment Cry Baby called *Fender Benders*. The paper carried notices about lost pets so Cry Baby instituted a program he named *Animal-A-Go-Go*. Obituaries? Cry Baby covered that with *Dead As A Doornail*.

The changes were going over well. So well, it seemed like everyone in Yuba City was talking about the new KLAS. That gave Cry Baby another idea. He started a call-in show hosted by Hoss, *The Pancake Club*, two hours in morning drive when people could phone in and vent. The telephone never stopped lighting up.

There were a few who nitpicked, mainly about the music. Country diehards who didn't appreciate having their musical horizons expanded.

The Sales Department, meanwhile, was bringing in bucks hand over iron fist. Revenue was up a whopping seven hundred percent. Part of that was due to Cry Baby's new sales pitch. All it usually took was a visit by Pretty Boy and Dill and business owners were glad to buy air time. Not only that, a lot of businesses that had been advertising on KWIN or KDLR were persuaded to switch to KLAS. So were businesses that formerly only ran ads in the newspaper.

All this filtered through Cry Baby's head as his limo neared his station.

"We're here, boss," Dill stated the obvious.

Cry Baby climbed out. The building was getting a new paint job. Since he couldn't tear it down and build a new one made of plastic and glass, he was doing the next best thing and have it painted so it looked like plastic and glass. Two painters were up on a scaffold, hard at work.

Cry Baby gave a cheery wave as he breezed under them and went inside, his wiseguys in a phalanx around him.

Meriam was at the front desk, sensational in a low-cut dress that stopped a cat's-whisker short of her nipples. "Morning, handsome. How's my studmuffin today?"

The sight of her made Cry Baby hard. But it was too early for a quickie so he asked, "Any calls?"

"Bunches. I left a pile on your desk. Tops is the mayor. He'd like you to buzz him back as soon as you can."

Strutting into his office, Cry Baby sank into the new plush chair that matched the new plush sofa. The mayor was a good old boy by the name of Wilkins. Cry Baby had bumped into him at *The Radison*. He picked up the phone and was put right through.

Wilkins was a fountain of bubbly charm. "Son, I have great news. As a token of gratitude for the outstanding job you're doing, the Chamber of Commerce is having a welcome-to-town banquet in your honor ten days from today. How would that be?"

Cry Baby said it was fine with him so long as they didn't expect him to foot the bill.

Wilkins cackled. "Lou, you're a caution. No, the Chamber pays for everything. All you have to do is show up, make a short speech, and try to look humble."

Cry Baby provoked more hilarity with, "I don't do humble. I'm too badass."

"Keep this up and I'll die laughing. Listen, Lou. We're

serious here. You're invigorating Yuba City. You've gotten everyone to sit up and take a look at who we are and be grateful for the good things we have. I'm not laying it on too thick when I say that your station is making us feel like we're all one big family."

"I'm big on Family," Cry Baby said.

"As well you should be. What I'm saying is, we were so used to the status quo, to the same old thing, day in and day out, that we needed someone like you to come along and give us a good shake. Stir things up, if you will. Like you've done with your music and all those new programs. I don't mind saying that you're a credit to our community."

Cry Baby hung up feeling like he could walk on water.

The second note on the stack was from Chief Poindexter. The chief had called to say the police had no clues as to what happened to Valentino and Misty Lane. Poindexter was of the opinion they'd eloped and he'd like to hear Cry Baby's thoughts.

Cry Baby chuckled. Poindexter rated a mention in the dictionary as the definition for stupider-than-shit. The chief had gone on record as saying leads were slim in the KDLR bombing. Explosive residue had been sent to a state lab to be tested but Poindexter wasn't optimistic it would lead to the culprits. As for the stolen transmitter, the police had chalked that up to a prank. They figured some college yo-yo's or high school kids were to blame.

Yeah, right, Cry Baby grinned as he tossed the note in the trash. He didn't need to worry about the Keystone Cops.

As for the notion that Val and the bimbo eloped, Cry Baby was of the opinion that there was no way a loverboy like Valentino would tie himself to one broad, expecially not a cornstalk cutie who didn't know squat about diddly. Cry Baby just couldn't see it. Not when Val could have his pick of any dame he wanted.

Yet if that was the case, where the hell were they?

Candy Girl warbled from the speakers and Cry Baby settled back to enjoy Frankie, but couldn't. His mind was locked on the Val thing. Maybe he should do as the Wolfman had suggested and call his old man. For a wiseguy to disappear was serious. Big Frank would no doubt put the Iceman on it.

Cry Baby Frowned. No, damn it. He didn't want the Iceman involved. They had issues. Besides, this was his station and his city and he'd handle his own problems. He'd had Switch nosing around, seeing if Val had been to any of the local night spots. So far Switch had struck out but Cry Baby was confident something would turn up.

For now, all Cry Baby wanted to do was bask in the glory of being treated like somebody important. It surprised him, how much he ate this stuff up, how much he liked running the radio station. He wouldn't have thought he had it in him. Maybe God was trying to tell him something. Maybe going legit was a good thing. In a year or so he might venture into politics, run for a council spot or throw his hat into the ring to replace the doofus mayor. From there, who knew? A bid for the state legislature, which in turn could be a stepping stone to the U.S. House or Senate. He'd be right at home there. Bossing people around, making rules everybody had to follow.

His father would be proud of him. Big Frank could brag to all the other dons about how his son was a by-God senator.

The morning passed quickly.

The president of Yuba City National called to invite him to the Yuba City Country Club. Was he interested in joining the Masons? the head of the local outfit wanted to know. The wealthiest couple in town, the Van Winkels, were throwing a party Friday night, and would Mr. Louis Scarvetti do them the honor of attending? How about taking part in the annual Toys for Tykes campaign? And say, every charity in town was in need of a donation---"Need we remind you it's tax deductible?"

By noon the executive routine had lost some of its luster. Cry Baby was glad to call it quits for a while and go grab a bite to eat.

Meriam was applying lipstick to those luscious lips of hers. She winked and said, "I'm randy as hell and proud of it."

Cry Baby did the gentlemanly thing. "Want to do lunch?"

Meriam jumped up. Her life had taken such an incredible turn for the better, she was half-afraid the bubble would burst. Being on her own for the first time in decades was thrilling. She marveled that she hadn't goaded Arty into blowing his brains out years ago.

CHAPTER THIRTY-FIVE

Meriam had arrived home the night of her first tryst with Cry Baby worn to a frazzle. Lou was the kind of man every woman longed for but few ever found. He'd been all over her like a starved bear on honey. And the great thing was, five minutes after he came, he was primed to go again. He'd laid her like a rug, in every orifice she had, as well as doing things to other parts of her body she'd never imagined could be used for that purpose. Her legs were wobbly when she snuck into the house. She'd figured Arty was so drunk he'd be dead to the world.

Instead, he was waiting for her.

Thank God Meriam had the foresight to send the kids to a friend's for the night or they would have heard Arty rant at her. He told her he'd always known about her antics, about the Oklahoma cowboy, about the pizza delivery boy, about the tennis pro, about the waitress at the diner. He called her every name in the book. Slut, whore, bitch, concubine. That last stumped her until she looked it up later.

Meriam had been too tired to argue. She let him foam at the mouth until he was foamed out, then she had shuffled down the hall, saying over her shoulder, "If you can't talk about this like a mature adult, we'll try again in the morning. Good night."

"Meriam."

Arty's voice never held such authority before. Meriam

had stopped and turned and saw the gun in his hand. He pointed it at her chest. "Oh, please," she'd scoffed. "You don't have the guts. If you were a real man, you never would have let the station slip through your fingers."

"Meriam, don't."

"Don't what? Tell it like it is?" Meriam shook a fist at him. "I should never have married you. If you had a shred of feeling for me, you'd turn that gun on yourself and do me and the rest of the world a favor."

"Go to hell."

"You're a loser. You'd never have amounted to anything without me."

"I ran a successful radio station."

"Successful? We barely stayed afloat. Oh, you had some spare change for your Vegas jaunts but that was it."

"What do you know?" Arty said bitterly.

Meriam gave it to him with both verbal barrels. "I know you're not a man in more ways than one. Especially in bed."

"Don't go there."

"I had to work so hard to get you up, I about lost interest by the time you were ready to dip your wick."

"You can be so crude."

"You're the worst fuck I ever had. That cowboy? He could fuck rings around you. Hell, Della at the diner fucks better than you do and she doesn't even have a dick."

Arty had raised the revolver to his head, the muzzle pressed against his temple. "I refuse to listen to any more of your bile."

Meriam's breath caught in her throat. She could have called out to him, could have told him she didn't mean it. Instead she said, "Give me a break. You don't have what it takes to squeeze that trigger."

"I can't stand this anymore," Arty said forlornly, and a tear trickled down his cheek.

"Prove it."

Damned if he didn't.

Meriam could forgive him for killing himself but not for the mess he made. He got blood all over their new carpet and hair and gore all over the wall and ceiling. The cleaning bill amounted to almost five hundred dollars.

But that was in the past. Now was now. Meriam smiled as she strolled arm-in-arm with Lou. His limo was at the curb. A UPS truck was parked in front of it. She could see the driver, scribbling whatever it was UPS drivers scribbled. She could be wrong but he looked Italian, the same as Cry Baby and his soldiers, as he called them. She thought that was funny.

CHAPTER THIRTY-SIX

As usual, Cry Baby's crew flanked him. Switch and the Wolfman were in the lead, Pretty Boy and Dill brought up the rear.

Switch was thinking about Val, about how he hoped his friend and the girl hadn't done what he suspected they'd done.

Dill was thinking about pickles and how he hadn't had one in at least an hour and a half.

The Wolfman was trying not to look at Meriam Johnson's ass.

As for Pretty Boy, he stared at the UPS truck. He'd noticed it ten or fifteen minutes ago when he stared out the office window. He thought it strange it was still there. They were almost to the curb when Pretty Boy saw the driver straighten, saw the man's lips move as if he were saying something. But no one else was in the cab.

The next moment the rear door to the truck was flung open and three men in suits hurtled out. Al three were armed with SMG's fitted with sound suppressors, MAC11's with cyclic rates of twelve hundred rounds a minute, each fitted with a 32-round box magazine.

"It's a hit!" Pretty Boy bawled, and grabbed for his Colt Python.

The triggermen had planned well. To take their quarry off-guard, they'd struck in broad daylight on Cry Baby's own turf, when and where he was least likely to expect it.

To ensure success, they'd caught him in the open so he had nowhere to take cover. Their choice of firepower was outright overkill. Instead of a single shot to the head by a sniper, they were going to shoot Cry Baby to ribbons to show the hit was personal.

As the triggermen spilled out, Switch was already in motion. Able to use both hands as fluidly as most people used one, he drew two switchblades simultaneously. At the flick of twin buttons, twin blades gleamed in the sunlight.

The first hitman was just stepping to the sidewalk when Switch threw one. He'd practiced the throw countless times and the knife streaked true, the cold steel slicing into the man's throat as he raised his MAC11. Momentum carried him forward a step, into the second switchblade, which imbedded itself in his chest.

Spouting blood, the man clutched at his neck, and died. In reflex, his finger tightened on the trigger and the MAC11 chugged. Slugs kicked up eruptions of dirt, stitching a path toward Switch. Switch dived and rolled.

By then the others had gone into action.

Pretty Boy banged off a shot that caught the second gunman in the shoulder and spun him around but didn't take him down. The man cursed and leveled his SMG, and Pretty Boy fired again, going for the head. The hollow point made a mess of the shooter's face.

The third hitman planted himself and opened fire, seeking to mow Pretty Boy down in order to have a clear shot at Cry Baby. But just then Dill lumbered into motion, unlimbering his Ruger Redhawk .44-Magnum. The burst meant for Pretty Boy slammed Dill back.

The third hitman skipped to the left for a better angle. It only took two seconds but in that span the Wolfman drew his pistol and squeezed off four shots, one of which pulverized the hitman's left eye.

In the truck cab, the driver saw his companions go down. He'd drawn an Auto-Ordnance Pit Bull but instead of using it, he turned the ignition key and put the pedal to the floor. The truck gained speed but not anywhere near fast enough. Trying to escape in it was like trying to escape in a giant brown turtle. Suddenly it stalled and lurched to a stop. Frantic, the driver twisted the key. The starter ground but the engine wouldn't kick over.

Cry Baby was furious at the try on his life. With a growl of rage he charged the truck, drawing his Astras.

Up and down the street vehicles honked and swerved. Women screamed. Men shouted and swore.

Cry Baby ran out in front of the truck just as the motor roared to life.

The driver spied him and tromped on the gas to run him down.

Cry Baby cut loose, firing both pistols, putting hole after hole in the windshield.

Jerking like a puppet on strings, the driver let go of the steering wheel. The truck veered into an oncoming pickup and there was a tremendous crash

In the distance sirens wailed.

CHAPTER THIRTY-SEVEN

To show how seriously the Ten Families took the Scola affair, nine of the ten sent representatives to Denver. The tenth Family wanted to be there but their upper echelon were busy with court appearances.

They came from all over. From New York, Atlanta, Detroit. Somber men in somber suits, their gravity not lost on Big Frank Scarvetti, who sat at one end of the long table with Dominick DeLuga, his consigliore.

At the other end sat Old Man Gambioso and his son, Armano.

Don Fabroni from Philadelphia was chosen to be spokesman for the Families not directly involved in the feud. He laid it on the line after both sides had presented their case.

"I'm sorry, Franco," Fabroni said. "You and I have known each other many years and shared many good times. But in this, Don Gambioso is in the right. We side with him."

"What is it you would have of me?" Big Frank asked. He was weary from lack of sleep and worn out from too much worry. This was the moment he'd dreaded and he struggled to keep his wits sharp.

Don Lorenz from Detroit stirred. He was one of the oldest and had a reputation for being fair in all his dealings. "You must understand our position, Don Scarvetti. We are men of strength, a strength based on the allegiance of those who serve us. That allegiance is based on rules of conduct. There are things our soldiers may do and things they may not do. When they obey, they are rewarded. When they disobey, when they break the rules, punishment must be swift and severe or the whole structure on which our strength is based will fall apart."

Don Giovanni cleared his throat. "What is the one ambition of every connected guy on the street? To be a made man. To earn his button. Why? It's one of the highest honors we bestow. A made man is of the inner circle. He has rights, he has privileges. One of them is that he can't be killed without the consent of his sponsor."

Big Frank spread his hands. "In this instance, as all of you know, my son was provoked."

Don Lorenz responded. "Provoked or not, he did wrong. I never met this Scola person, and from what I hear, I wouldn't like him if I had. But the fact remains. Scola was a made man with the Gambioso Family and your son killed him without permission. If we let your son get away with it, what is to stop others from thinking they can get away with the same thing? In no time our strength will erode and we would be no better than the pezzonovantis we despise.'

"I ask again," Big Frank said. "What is it you want of me?"

Old Man Gambioso broke his silence. "An eye for an eye. The life of your son for Vic Scola."

Big Frank looked at each of the other Dons. Some showed sympathy but every last one nodded when he looked at them. He felt an invisible fist close around his chest, and squeeze.

"That's not all," Old Man Gambioso went on. "Your son's crew was with him when it happened. They share his guilt. Their lives, too, are forfeit."

Big Frank stiffened. "You ask too much. They weren't involved. One of them even tried to talk my son out of it. Punishing them would be as wrong as it was for my son to whack Scola."

His friend, Don Fabroni, bent forward and said sadly, "We disagree, Franco. We've talked it over. We must make an example of them. An object lesson. So no one in any of our organizations will think to do anything like this ever again." He glanced at his watch. "We realize what we're asking. We'll give you an hour to think it over and give us your decision. Should you refuse---." He didn't finish. He didn't need to.

The meeting was being held at the Denver Hilton. Big Frank told DeLuga to stay in the conference room and went up to their suite. Claws of raw emotion tore at his insides. His son. His precious son. He'd rather lose all he had than lose Little Lou.

The Iceman was on the couch, immersed in a *Reader's Digest*. He immediately put it down. "How bad?"

"They want Lou and all his crew."

"His crew? I didn't expect that."

Big Frank poured himself a whiskey and began to pace. He related what the Commission members had said, ending with, "It'll be a cold day in hell before I give in. I'll go to war against all of them if I have to."

"Everything you've worked so hard to build will be lost."

Big Frank stopped pacing and a look of great sorrow came over him. "It's my son, Enzo. What else can I do?"

"You should sit down. I have something to tell you, Franco. Something I should have told you long ago."

Big Frank sank into a chair.

"You're aware that your son and I are on the outs and have been for some time," the Iceman said. "Have you wondered why?"

"I've noticed you can't stand to be around him, yes. But there are times when I can't stand to be around him, myself. He's my flesh and blood but he can be a pain."

"That's not why I dislike him." The Iceman frowned. "About a year and a half ago Louis showed up at my door. He was plastered, so drunk he could hardly stand. He said he had a job for me. I told him I only do your bidding. He said he would pay me more than I earned on any job, ever."

"Lou wanted to hire you to do a hit? Who did he want killed?"

The Iceman took off his Aviator shades. His grey eyes were sad. "Your son wanted me to whack you."

Franco Scarvetti's world burst into shards and rained down around him. He set his drink on the end table, balled his big fists, and hugged his belly as if he were ill. "God, Enzo. No. Please, no."

"He said he wanted to be the head of the Family sooner rather than later. That if I helped him, I could be his chief enforcer as I was yours."

"What did you do?"

"I grabbed him and took him out on the balcony and held him over the rail. I told him you were my best friend. I said that I would kill myself before I'd kill you." The Iceman paused. "I vowed that son or no son, I'd gladly do him if he ever tried to have you whacked. And I made him promise not to say a word to anyone about our talk."

"You should have told me."

"I kept silent to spare you. I know how much you love

him."

"All I've done for him, and he did that?"

"Like I say, he was drunk. I doubt he knew what he was doing. He might not even remember it."

"Whether he does or he doesn't hardly matters. It changes everything."

"I'm sorry, Franco."

Big Frank did something he hadn't done since he was eight years old. He wept.

Forty-five minutes later he stood up in the conference room and declared, "I agree to your request. For the common good of us all, my son and his crew will be sacrificed."

If any of the other dons noticed a slight puffiness to his eyes or how his voiced quavered, they kept it to themselves.

"I only ask that you consent to let me handle this myself. As a personal favor to me."

All eyes swung toward Old Man Gambioso. Rising, he came down the table and embraced Big Frank. The rest applauded. Fences had been mended. Open war had been averted.

Old Man Gambioso silenced them with a gesture. "We are grateful that Don Scarvetti has agreed to our terms. I am not without feelings and my heart goes out to him. I, too, have a son, and I know what he must be going through."

Big Frank looked down at his shoes.

"As a token of my good will, and out of gratitude for the courage he has shown here this day, I have something for him." Old Man Gambioso reached into a pocket and held up a tape. "Ever since the Feds tried to entrap me by tapping my phones, I have recorded all calls to and from my various enterprises."

"How does that relate to this?" Don Fabroni asked.

"A call was received at my olive oil company." Old Man Gambioso held the tape out to Big Frank. "It's my gift to you. As a token of my appreciation."

"I don't understand," Big Frank said, accepting it. "What is on here that would be of interest to me?"

"A traitor in your Family."

CHAPTER THIRTY-EIGHT

Eddy the Book lived in a plush suite on the twelfth floor of *The Golden Nugget*. He liked the convenience of being close to his office. A short elevator ride and he was home, as it were. Most nights, like this one, he unlocked the door and hurried in to catch *Seinfeld*. A local station was airing reruns.

The show was Eddy's pet passion, his antidote to the pressures of his job. After ten to twelve hours of dealing with intricate financial problems, it was a joy to relax and laugh at the antics of Jerry and the gang. The show was outrageous yet so real. It reminded him of his childhood, the time when he was happiest. He'd known guys like meathead George and crazies like Kramer.

The truth be known, though, he mainly watched it for Elaine. He didn't have a wife, didn't have a girlfriend. Having one would be nice but he spent so much time at the casino, he rarely got to meet likely prospects. The women who worked at the Nugget didn't appeal to him. What he wanted was a nice Jewish girl. A girl like Elaine. A girl who could be warm and witty and sexy. Eddy worshipped her. He liked to daydream of him and her doing the down and dirty. If only.

Eddy was in such a rush to turn on the TV, he headed across the room without turning on the lights. He'd taken half a dozen steps when it dawned on him that the carpet had a strange feel even as his ears registered a peculiar crinkling sound, like a plastic garbage bag being unraveled.

Light flooded the room.

Eddy stopped in mixed horror and shock. His blood froze in his veins. Sheets of plastic covered the living room floor and Big Frank was in a chair, his legs crossed, his big hands spread on the chair's arms.

The Iceman stood next to a lamp he'd just switched on. He held a pistol with a suppressor attached.

"I want to know why, Ed," Big Frank said.

"Why what?" Eddy the Book replied. But he knew. God help him, he knew.

"You, of all people. We grew up together. I protected you from the bullies in school. We went on double-dates. You were a groomsman at my wedding. So please. I'd very much like to know why."

Eddy felt surprisingly calm. Great regret, great fear, but calm. As if he'd always known a day like this would come and long ago he'd subconsciously accepted the fact. He didn't ask how in the world Big Frank found out. It was unimportant. "I did it because of my deep affection for you. Because he's rotten to the core. Because one day he'll bring you down and I wanted to save you from that."

"There was no need. They've decided it must be a life for a life. You should have stuck to juggling figures and not gotten involved." Big Frank exhaled, deflating like a balloon. He seemed much older than he had a week ago. "I saw the clippings you left on my desk. About the mark's suicide, the tower that was blown up, the whole mess. About the hit by the Gambiosos before the sit-down in Denver. I thank you for them."

"I really do care," Eddy the Book said.

"I know." Big Frank closed his eyes. "Enzo."

There was a *thwip*.

Big Frank opened his eyes. Eddy the Book lay in a sprawl on the plastic. "I loved him like a brother."

The Iceman walked over and fired twice more into Eddy the Book's head. "I liked him, too."

Big Frank stood and tiredly rubbed his eyes. "Have Ronco's crew take care of the body. I want you in Yuba City by morning."

"Your son and his crew?"

"Everyone involved, Enzo. And I mean everyone."

"Anything special? Or make them all clean?"

"Clean all around. His crew deserves that much. I don't want them to suffer. The important thing is that no loose ends are left alive. Not a single one."

"Consider it done," the Iceman said.

CHAPTER THIRTY-NINE

Chief of Police Lexter Poindexter was an early riser. He liked to get up at the crack of dawn. It came from being raised on a ranch. The morning chores couldn't wait. Cows had to be milked, manure shoveled, the hogs and chickens fed. All before breakfast.

His clock alarm went off at five and he shut it off before it woke his wife. He rubbed his Adam's-apple and listened to her snore. She could shake the walls, his Alice.

Suddenly Chief Poindexter gave a start.

The glow from the nightlight revealed a man in dark glasses standing by the side of the bed. In his befuddled, still-sleepy state, Chief Poindexter thought it must be one of his deputies. "Harve? Is that you? What are you doing here?"

"It's not Harve," the Iceman said. He raised his pistol and centered the silencer on Poindexter's forehead. "You've been making inquiries of certain state and federal agencies about the new owner of the radio station. We pay snitches to inform us when that happens."

Poindexter came fully alert. "Hold on," he blurted. "You can't kill a law officer."

The Iceman tilted his head. "I've probably heard it before but I'll bite. Why not?"

"You shoot one of us," Poindexter said, "every lawman in the country will be after you."

"You've never seen Scarface, I take it?"

"Sorry?" Poindexter said. He glanced at his gunbelt. He always placed it on a dresser near the bed within easy reach. Only now did he realize that three feet might as well be three miles.

"It's a movie the son of my employer likes to watch. The point is that your badge isn't the same as a bright red S."

"Sorry?" Poindexter said again.

The Iceman nodded at the dresser. "You can try for it if you want."

Poindexter did. He was thinking maybe the hitman would miss, maybe he could grab his piece and nail the bastard before the bastard nailed him. He was thinking that when he heard a muffled sound and the room went dark.

Alice Poindexter rolled over with an annoyed grunt. "Les? What's all the commotion? You know better than to wake me." She saw her husband lying half in and half out of the bed, saw a man she didn't know train a gun on her. "Hold on!" she shrieked. "What's this about?"

"Some husbands tell their wives everything." The Iceman shot her between the eyes and once more in the temple after she collapsed.

He was wearing gloves so he wasn't worried about prints as he took their phone from the night stand. He'd already looked up the number he wanted and tapped it.

"Yuba City Police Department. May I help you?"

The Iceman was good at disguising his voice. He disguised it now. "Get to your chief's house right away."

"What was that?"

"Your chief has been shot. Him and his wife, both." The Iceman broke the connection and left. Every cop in town would respond to that call. Which left the rest of Yuba City wide open.

The emergency exit on the ground floor of Yuba General Hospital wasn't locked. The Iceman glided up the stairwell to the fourth floor, cracked the door, and made sure the corridor was empty. It wouldn't be for long. In half an hour the day shift would arrive. He needed to work fast.

His hand under his jacket, the Iceman stalked down the hall. He'd phoned to confirm the room, pretending to be a relative. Voices gave him pause.

A stout nurse had her hands on her hips and was grinning at her patient. "Honestly, I don't know how I let you talk me into this, Mr. Simone. I could get into trouble, you know."

"For bringing me a jar of pickles?" Dill was in bed, propped on pillows, a sheet up to his waist, his right arm and upper chest bandaged. "Cindy, you're my kind of gal. When I get out of here, you and me are doing the town." He tried to open the jar one-handed.

Giggling, the nurse took it. "Here. Let me. You'll start bleeding again."

The Iceman watched her remove the cap. He watched Dill dip two big fingers into the jar and slide a pickle out. He waited for the right moment, for the instant when Dill popped the pickle in his mouth and closed his eyes and heavenly delight spread across his face.

"Cindy, you have no idea how much I've missed these."

Stepping into the room, the Iceman put two slugs into Dill's head.

Cindy the nurse jumped and raised a hand to her throat. She thrust out her other hand as the pistol swung toward her. "No! Please! All I did was give him pickles."

"Wrong place, wrong time," the Iceman said, and squeezed the trigger twice. He didn't bother with the ejected shell casings. He'd worn gloves when he loaded the clips and the ammo was a common brand sold throughout the United States. The gun itself was a .22. Not much for stopping power but that was why he double-tapped. He turned to go, and glanced at Dill and frowned.

"Hell," the Iceman said.

CHAPTER FORTY

The morning rush hour traffic was heavy. Deep in thought, the Iceman hardly noticed.

Enzo didn't like this job. It bothered him, and jobs weren't supposed to bother him. He couldn't let them. He'd spent years mastering his emotions, suppressing them, cramming them into a vault in the depths of his being where they were to stay locked. But they were scratching at the vault door, and it troubled him.

Enzo had a special talent for two things, controlling his feelings and killing. The control he'd learned courtesy of an alcoholic father. Stefano Taza had been a hulking dockworker whose wife left him over his drinking and his temper, so Stefano turned his spite on his son, beating Enzo nearly every day, beating him for slights of conduct and beating him for the hell of it.

Enzo was eleven when he had decided enough was enough. Prior to that, he'd always cried when his father hit him. He'd cry and beg his father to stop. His father never did. Then came the day when Enzo vowed he'd never cry again. He wouldn't ever show weakness.

It made Stefano madder. He went into frenzies, hitting Enzo with a belt or a stick to make him shed tears. Enzo learned to block out the hurt. His eyes stayed dry.

Enzo had one friend his own age. Franco Scarvetti. By the time they were twelve, Franco had started down a road made of blood-red bricks. Franco became attached to the neighborhood wiseguys. He ran errands for them, he delivered messages. Franco tried to talk Enzo into working with him but Enzo declined. It would give his father another excuse to beat him.

Then one night Enzo was on the roof, taking care of his pigeons. Stefano appeared, drunk as usual, and mad that Enzo hadn't washed the dishes after supper. Stefano cursed him and hit him and grabbed a pigeon Enzo was holding.

"You and these stupid birds. I'm sick of them and I'm sick of you." Stefano had wrung the pigeon's neck. Laughing savagely, he'd stepped to the edge to throw the dead bird into the street.

Enzo pushed his father off. Stefano was so besotted, he didn't cry out or scream. Enzo saw the body strike the sidewalk, saw the splat of the head and the spray of blood. Turning, he'd descended to their apartment. He was washing the dishes when the police knocked. They were kind to him, saying wasn't it a shame his old man was such a boozer that he'd taken a header off the roof while fooling with the pigeons.

Enzo was sent to live with an aunt who lived only a few blocks away. The very next day he went to work with Franco. They never spoke of Stefano but Franco knew. From then on, whenever Franco had a problem that couldn't be solved, he relied on Enzo. Enzo didn't mind. He'd felt nothing when he killed his father, and he trained himself to feel nothing when he killed others.

There were a few instances, though. Like the time he chopped up Finelli's wife. Franco had wanted her chopped up alive. The mess was terrible. But it was her face, her eyes, her constant whimpering that got to him. It was shortly after doing her that he took to killing puppies and kittens to harden himself and purge his weakness.

Now this new job.

Wiseguys who went bad, who squealed to the cops or skimmed money, Enzo could whack all day and all night and not feel a thing. He'd experienced regret when he shot Eddy the Book but that was because Eddy had hooked up with Franco shortly after he did. The three of them had been the Three Musketeers. They rose through the ranks together, reached the pinnacle together. Killing Eddy wasn't easy.

Enzo felt no regrets about having to do Cry Baby. He looked forward to it. He relished the thought of whacking him more than he'd relished the prospect of any hit, ever. He didn't relish doing Cry Baby's crew. They hadn't done anything wrong. They were like that nurse. They'd been in the wrong place at the wrong time. They'd been there when Cry Baby caved Vic Scola's head in. Killing them wasn't right. But those were his personal feelings and personal feelings were of no consequence when he had a job to do.

A sign let Enzo know he was on the right road. He drove into a parking lot adjacent to Yuba City Memorial Park. At that hour few people were abroad. A couple of joggers, and a woman walking her poodle, none of them close enough to see his face.

Enzo recalled the reporter's directions and moved along a path bordered by trees.

Tim Sattler, investigative reported for the *Yuba City Tribune*, was waiting on a park bench. A briefcase was at his feet. He stood when Enzo approached.

"Mr. Smith, isn't it? I don't see why you had to call me in the middle of the night to set this up. But I'll be glad to take a look at whatever evidence you have linking Louis Scarvetti to organized crime. I take it you've seen the articles I've written on him already?"

"We've seen them," Enzo said. He drew his pistol and pointed the suppressor at the reporter's head and fired twice. Using his foot, he rolled the body under the bench after first checking each pocket to be sure Sattler didn't have a note on him about the phone call. He took Sattler's wallet, and the briefcase.

The woman walking the poodle had drifted close to his car. She smiled a friendly smile. "Morning." Taking a deep breath she happily declared, "It's a great day to be alive, isn't it?"

"For some of us," the Iceman said, and shot her. The poodle, too. He climbed in the car and drove off.

The radio was on, and the Iceman caught a KLAS news bulletin to the effect that the police chief and his wife had been found dead in their home and a nurse and a patient had been murdered at the hospital.

Wait until they find out about the park, Enzo thought.

Yuba City didn't know it but this was just the start.

CHAPTER FORTY-ONE

Susie Q and Duke were in the break room, Susie eating a donut, Duke with a coffee.

Susie had gone to the police station earlier to find out if anything newsworthy had occurred overnight. It was standard practice with police departments to let radio and TV reporters and print journalists read edited versions of the official log, and from it Susie learned about the police chief and the hospital victims. She'd rushed back to KLAS to get it on the air. That done, she was licking the glaze off her breakfast while listening to Duke.

"I'm telling you, I don't like it. We should skedaddle while the skedaddlin' is good. Before that no-account coyote and those varmints he calls associates show up."

Talking with her mouth crammed with donut was difficult but Susie managed. "You want me to up and quit? Walk out when I don't have another job lined up? And then what? Go on welfare?"

Duke drummed the fingers of both hands on the table. "Are you addlepated, woman? Haven't I been warning you for days? That shootout out front, the chief stopping by, and now he's dead and that feller in the hospital and his nurse gunned down. It's all tied to that polecat we work for. If we don't light a shuck we're liable to be next."

"What have we done that someone would want to kill us?" Susie asked skeptically.

"We're workin' for that Scarvetti hombre."

"No one is going to kill us over that."

The Iceman had listened to enough. He'd slipped into the station through the rear door and the break room was the first room he came to. He walked in, saying, "I wouldn't be so sure." They turned, and Enzo put two slugs into the woman. She collapsed onto the table, bits of donut dribbling from her mouth.

"You son of a bitch," Duke snarled. "She was my gal." Heaving out of his chair, he flew at the Iceman in a rage.

Enzo cored his brain twice and stepped aside as the lifeless husk pitched past. He replaced the partially spent clip and moved on.

There had been little noise. The radio station was quiet save for a Frankie Valli song issuing from the speakers.

The next door had SALES stenciled on it. Slowly twisting the knob, the Iceman cracked it open. Two men were at separate desks, doing paperwork. The older of the pair was talking.

"---can't take much more of this. Did you see what they did to Charlie Gavin when he refused to advertise with us? That could be you and me, Billy, if we don't sell as many spots as that crazy bastard wants."

"What do we do?" the younger one asked. "Go to the police?"

"I will if you go with me."

"I don't know, Sam," Billy said. "That Scarvetti and his thugs scare me."

The Iceman entered. "Smart man," he said. He shot the older one and then the young one, both in the head, and shot them again for good measure as they lay on the floor.

The next room had a sign that read PRODUCTION. Above the sign was a red light that was glowing. Under the sign was a typed note: *When this light is on, someone is recording. Please don't enter until the light goes out.*

Enzo poked his head in.

A guy in jeans and a blue shirt was seated on a stool at a console, in front of a microphone. In a remarkable display of mimicry, he said just like Tweety Bird, "If you twaught you knew bwargains, you don't, Vwist Qwuality Chwrevolet for cwool dweals." He tweaked a knob and a jingle blared. "For top dollar savings, Quality is the place." Smiling, he turned another knob and said to himself, "Got it on the first take."

The man stood and glanced over his shoulder and saw the Iceman. "Who in the world are you?"

"You first," the Iceman said, entering, his pistol behind his leg .

"I'm Larry Todd, the Program Director. Didn't you see that red light over the door? If you'd made a noise while I was recording, you would have spoiled the commercial I was doing." He turned. "Are you that reporter who's been wanting to talk to me? You'll have to wait. I've called a special meeting of the staff in twenty minutes about all the stuff that's been going down."

"So it's you I should thank for gathering all the eggs in one basket."

"I beg your pardon?"

The Iceman drilled Larry Todd twice in the forehead. Todd fell, pulling the stool down with him. The Iceman went over to confirm the kill.

Suddenly the door swung open again and in strode a man carrying a circuit tester and prattling away. "Larry, you in here? What the hell is so important that I had to come all the way in from the---." He stopped, his eyes widening.

The Iceman covered him. He didn't like how close the guy was to the door so he motioned. "Shut it and take a step toward me."

His eyes glued to the pistol, the man complied.

"Who are you?" the Iceman asked. "What do you do here?"

"H---H---Howard Branigan," the man stuttered. "I'm the Chief Engineer." He stared at Larry Todd and started to tremble. "No."

"Yes," the Iceman said, and added a chief engineer to his string.

CHAPTER FORTY-TWO

Cry Baby and his crew---what was left of it---didn't arrive at KLAS until ten past nine. Meriam was with them. She'd spent the night at The Radison with Cry Baby.

Hoss was on the air. His last hourly newscast had mentioned, yet again, the deaths of Dill and the police chief.

Cry Baby went straight to the control room to get the news copy. He wanted to read it for himself.

Everything had gone to hell and Cry Baby knew who to blame. The damn Gambiosos. Their failed hit had broken his string of luck. The cops were on his case, the newspaper was digging up all the dirt it could on him, and he was persona non grata among Yuba City's shakers and movers. The mayor had called to say the welcome-to-town banquet was cancelled. The visit to the Yuba City Country Club was off. And then there was the six-figure bail he'd had to post for his arrest over his part in the shootout with the fake UPS driver and the triggermen.

Switch, Pretty Boy and the Wolfman followed him into the office. All three were on edge. Dill's death had hit them hard.

"The fucking Gambiosos," Cry Baby said. "They tried to whack me, they whacked Dill in the hospital. Smart money says they whacked Val and the bimbo, too."

Meriam walked in. She'd rather not be there. She would rather never set foot in the radio station ever again. The gun battle the other day had shown her she was in over her head. Dallying with Mobsters had drawbacks she hadn't foreseen. Violent drawbacks.

But she couldn't come right out and tell Lou she didn't want to work for him anymore. Not when he was in one of his moods. Just last night she'd mentioned it might be smart for him to head back to Vegas and he'd slapped her so hard, he'd knocked her down. The feral gleam in his eyes as he stood over her had scared like nothing else ever had.

"These Gambioso people you keep talking about," Meriam now said. "Will they try to murder me, too?"

"I would if I was them,"Cry Baby said. "What do you want, bitch? I told you no more calls."

Meriam checked a sharp retort. "I thought you might want something to eat. We didn't have breakfast, if you'll recall. Susie always has extra donuts, and I can get you one if you want."

"What the hell does food matter with the Gambiosos making war on me?" Cry Baby gestured. "Go feed your face, slutbox. I need to think." He added as an afterthought as she wheeled on a heel. "Bring something for my crew, though."

"Thanks, Mr. Scarvetti," the Wolfman said.

"Who asked you, furface?"

Out in the hall, Meriam stomped toward the break room. The nerve of that bastard, talking to her like that. There was only so much abuse she'd put up with. For all of Arty's flaws, one thing he never did was hit her. She'd never appreciated how kind Arty was to her until now. For the first time since he blew his brains out, she truly and genuinely missed him.

Meriam was almost to the production room when she

noticed a dark liquid seeping from under the door. Puzzled, she stopped. The liquid was red. Not the red of wine or the red of a power drink. It almost looked like blood. Squatting, she touched the tip of a finger to it, and sniffed. It was blood.

"What in the world?" Meriam straightened and opened the door. Without warning she was shoved from behind and propelled into the room. Her foot caught on something and she came down hard on her knees. Belatedly, her mind registered two bodies.

"Oh God," Meriam bleated as a man in Aviator glasses entered. He was holding a pistol. Fear gripped her and she gasped, "Are you one of the Gambiosos?"

"No," the Iceman answered, and studied her. "Who are you, exactly?"

Meriam told him.

"Arty Johnson's wife? How do you know about the Gambiosos?"

Meriam was thinking furiously. Lou had said that his father might send someone to help them. This must be him. But then, why were Larry Todd and Howard Branigan lying there dead? "Lou told me all about them. Did Big Frank send you?"

"That idiot never did know when to keep his mouth shut." The Iceman extended his pistol.

Recoiling, Meriam exclaimed, "Wait. I don't want to die."

"Who does?"

Meriam hitched at her skirt. "If you let me live I'll make it worth your while. There's nothing I won't do. Nothing at all."

"I don't sleep with women."

"How in the world can you go without? That's not normal."

The Iceman shot her twice in the mouth and twice more in the forehead. He replaced the clip, slipped the pistol under his jacket, and went down the hall past the control room, ignoring the DJ. He'd do him last.

He had others to do first.

CHAPTER FORTY-THREE

In the office Switch stepped to the coffee maker. He needed a jolt of caffeine, and needed it bad. He was tired from not enough sleep and when a wiseguy was tired he lost his edge. "Anyone else want a cup?"

"I'll take one," Pretty Boy said. He could use something stronger but coffee would have to do. Dill's death had gotten to him. They'd worked well together and were often paired off and he'd grown fond of the big gorilla. A dumb gorilla, true, but someone he could count on when their backs were to the wall. To take his mind off Dill being whacked, he admired himself in the mirror.

"One for me, too, if you don't mind," the Wolfman said. He was leaning against a wall, in the dumps. Their crew, his family within the Family, was being decimated. Val missing, Dill dead. What next? he wondered.

That was when the Iceman casually strolled in. "The cavalry has arrived," he announced with a rare smile.

Switch, Pretty Boy and the Wolfman all spun. When they saw who it was they grinned and relaxed.

"Iceman!" the Wolfman said happily. "Is Big Frank with you?" He gazed over the chief enforcer's shoulder, eager to see the one who always solved their problems.

"It's just me," the Iceman said. "Mr. Scarvetti sent me to deal with the situation."

Pretty Boy chuckled. "Brother, are we glad to see you. A lot has been going down around here and none of it good." He glanced into the mirror and beamed in relief.

Switch indicated the coffee pot. "Can I interest you in some java?"

"No thanks," the Iceman said.

Cry Baby stayed in his chair at his desk. "My old man sent you? Why didn't he come himself? Hasn't he been keeping up on things?"

"He's been keeping up," the Iceman said.

"The Family needs to go to the mats," Cry Baby said. "The fucking Gambiosos have declared war. We have to plan, him and me. We have to work out what to do."

"He already has."

"How's that?" Cry Baby said.

"The sit-down in Denver," the Iceman said. "The parties involved have come to an agreement."

"What kind of agreement? And why the hell hasn't pops called to fill me in?"

"He sent me to explain things," the Iceman said, moving to a spot where he could see all four of them at the same time.

"Did my father lay down the law and tell the Gambiosos to go fuck themselves?"

The Iceman steeled himself. "The other Dons laid down the law to him, I'm afraid."

"Laid down the law how?"

"Your father agreed to their terms, Louis. Especially after I told him about you wanting me to whack him."

Switch and Pretty Boy and the Wolfman all glanced at Cry Baby in disbelief.

"You told him?" Cry Baby said, blanching and coming out of his chair. "You stupid fuck. Why would you do that to me?"

"Do you really need to ask?"

Placing his fists on his desk, Cry Baby glowered in fury. "What did he say when you told him? Why the fuck are you here, exactly?"

The Iceman concentrated on the other three. In all the years he'd been an enforcer, he'd never done what he did next. He looked at each of them and said, "I'm sorry."

"Sorry for what?" Pretty Boy asked.

"You don't deserve this," the Iceman said, and drew and shot Pretty Boy in the head. He spun and put a slug where the Wolfman's bushy eyebrows met and spun again toward Switch.

God, Switch was fast. The Iceman had shot the first two in the blink of an eye but the blond wiseguy was already moving. Switch dived to the right, twin switchblades appearing as if by magic in his hands. It forced the Iceman to rush his shot and in his haste he did something else he'd never done before. He missed.

A switchblade streaked at the Iceman's throat. He threw himself aside and felt a sting and the wet of blood. It was the first wound anyone ever inflicted on him. He chugged off a shot and this time clipped Switch but it wasn't enough.

Switch let fly with the second switchblade.

The Iceman twisted and the knife missed him by a hair. Had he been a fraction slower, it would have sliced into his eye. He fired as Switch swooped his hands to his special vest, fired as Switch pumped his arm for another throw, fired as Switch fell.

"What the fuck?" Cry Baby cried. He was riveted in astonishment. "You just whacked my fucking crew!" He shook a fist. "Wait until my father finds out, you fucking moron."

"Slow on the take, as always," the Iceman said, and shot Cry Baby in the elbow.

Shock more than pain caused Cry Baby to stagger back. He recovered and swore and clawed with his other hand for an Astra.

The Iceman shot him in the other elbow.

Cry Baby cried out and clutched his arms in agony. "You miserable son of a bitch," he screamed.

The Iceman shot him in the thigh.

With a howl of rage, Cry Baby launched himself toward the door. Two quick shots, one to each knee, brought him crashing down. "Fuck! Fuck! Fuck!"

The Iceman walked over to him.

Cry Baby's limbs were next to useless but he wriggled for the door until a shoe slammed onto his back, pinning him. Clenching his teeth against the waves of pain, he looked up into the dark hole at the end of the silencer. "You can't do this."

"I do what your father tells me."

"You're lying. I want to talk to him. You hear me? Get him on the phone."

"That's not going to happen."

Cry Baby's head was spinning so that he could hardly think. "This can't be happening,."

"You stepped in it when you whacked Scola," the Iceman said. "Disrespect the rules and you disrespect those who make them. Your father tried to warn you but you wouldn't listen. You never listened."

"He wouldn't," Cry Baby insisted. He closed his eyes, not from the pain, but so the Iceman wouldn't see the tears that were forming.

"It's up to me how long it takes," the Iceman said. "I could cap you in the head and get it over with. But you're going to be a good long while dying."

"Bastard. You never did like me, not even when I was little."

"I never liked all the grief you gave your father."

"Go to hell."

The pressure on Cry Baby's back went away. He heard the Iceman move off, and looked. The enforcer was bending over Switch. The Iceman slid a switchblade from the special vest, pressed a button, and cold steel gleamed. "What are you doing?"

The Iceman came back. "Ever been carved on? The hurt doesn't stop until the very end."

"I deserve better, damn you."

The Iceman squatted and held the tip of the blade close to Cry Baby's right eye. "You deserve what you get. But before we start I have a question. Tell me what I want to know and I might go easier on you. Refuse to talk, and, well." The Iceman shrugged.

Cry Baby's throat was so dry he had to try twice to say, "What's the question?"

"Where's Valentino?"

"Oh God," Cry Baby said.

CHAPTER FORTY-FOUR

Misty Lane had found something that scared her to the bone. Something that scared her more than abandoning her parents. Something that scared her more than leaving everyone and everything she knew. Something that scared her more than Val's stories about the Mafia and what the Mafia would do to them if they were caught.

That something was Los Angeles.

Misty had read about L.A. She'd seen L.A. on TV and in the movies. But none of that prepared her for the real L.A..

The city was a horror, a hideous sprawling monster with millions of heads and mouths and limbs. The foul air, the press of people, the congested traffic, assaulted her senses, battering her, leaving her bewildered.

Misty didn't want to be there. She longed for the peace and relative quiet of Yuba City.

She was a small town girl and she liked a small town atmosphere. She liked order, and people who were polite and considerate.

L.A. was the opposite. It was chaos. Its inhabitants had refined rudeness to an art. They honked at her or flipped a finger if she didn't drive fast enough. When she walked down the street they ogled her or made rude comments. They offered to sell her illegal substances, right out in the open.

Misty would rather hide out somewhere in the country

but Val insisted the best place was a large city. There was safety in numbers, he'd told her. In L.A. they were two specks in a seething sea of humanity, or as she liked to think of it, two needles in a gigantic hay stack.

Logically, Val's argument made sense. Emotionally, Misty was hard pressed to adapt.

Their apartment was in a run-down building where the renters were packed in like sardines. The halls were murky and dirty, many of the lights were broken, the walls were cracked and covered with graffiti. And there were smells, awful smells that made her hold her breath so as not to smell them. Worst of all, though, were the cries and oaths and screams that filled the building at all hours of the day and night but mostly at night.

Small wonder Misty stayed locked in their apartment whenever Val was gone. She sat on the worn couch and watched the small portable TV or gazed out their grimy window at the slice of L.A. visible below. She never tired of studying the parade of creatures who skulked by. Gang members who wore what Val called their 'colors', strutting like roosters in a barnyard. Younger kids, gang wannabes, who swaggered and smoked and treated each other like punching bags. Older people who walked with their backs bent and their heads bowed, as if by shutting out the world, the world would leave them alone.

Val assured her they wouldn't be there long, that as soon as he took care of a few things, they'd go somewhere nice. It couldn't happen soon enough to suit her.

Misty refused to venture outside unless Val was with her even though there was a convenience store on the corner and he'd given her plenty of money for snacks and magazines. She'd gone there once alone and it was one time too many. Several toughs gave her a hard time. They made insulting suggestions and one had brazenly rubbed against her. She'd bowed her head like the old people did, and ran. Thankfully, they didn't come after her.

Misty didn't tell Val. She knew what he would do.

Then came the cruelest shock of all.

Misty happened to be watching the news when a special bulletin came on. Her interest perked when Yuba City was mentioned. She listened in horror to what the newsman called 'a slaughter'. Subsequent reports labeled it the worst Mob warfare since the days of Al Capone. Over twenty people had been killed, and two dogs. Most had been shot execution-style.

Val told her it was the Mafia's way of cleaning house. Tidying up loose ends, he said. He claimed one man was responsible for all the deaths. Just one man.

Misty burst into tears when photos of some of the radio station staff were shown. Publicity stills of Susie Q, Duke and Hoss. The latter had been killed in the control room toward the end of his shift. Apparently, a song ended and he hadn't come back on. Nothing but dead air until a woman from a local diner came to update the ad copy on her weekly specials and discovered the station littered with bodies. The poor woman had suffered a breakdown.

As horrifying as the murders were, it shocked Misty more to realize that if she had been there, she'd be dead, too. She'd never given much thought to dying but she gave it a lot of thought after those news reports.

Now, her legs curled under her, Misty lay on the couch, her head propped on a ragged pillow. The gold ring on her finger caught her eye. It was really there. She was really married. She thought it cost too much but Val said it wasn't expensive enough, that she deserved better. He vowed that once they were on their feet financially, he'd buy her a ring that put this one to shame.

They weren't exactly broke. Between her savings and the money Val had socked away, they had nine thousand dollars to their name.

Val called it a pittance. About half would go toward buying them new identities, forged birth certificates and licenses and social security cards. The rest they'd use to start their new lives.

The TV droned on about the latest political scandal in Washington, D.C. Misty closed her eyes and let herself drift off, the wedding ring pressed to her cheek.

She dreamed that she was walking along L.A. streets shrouded with pollution as thick as fog. Footsteps sounded behind her, and loud breathing. Panicked, she ran, fleeing for their apartment. The fog confused her. She couldn't figure out which way to go. Dashing madly this way and that, she heard the footsteps grow louder, the breathing come closer. Just when she was sure whoever was after her was about to grab her, she woke up with a start.

For a few seconds Misty couldn't make sense of what she was seeing. She thought she must be dreaming. But no, in the shadows near the door stood a man in a black suit, wearing sunglasses. She sat up. "Val? You're back sooner than you'd said you'd be."

The man stepped out holding a pistol with a silencer. "It's not Valentino, Ms. Lane." He came almost to the couch, and stopped.

Misty gasped. Her dream had been a harbinger. Death had come to claim her in the guise of the Grim Reaper. Not the old-fashioned kind with a robe and a scythe but a modern Reaper in a tailored suit and glittering dark glasses. "You're him, aren't you? The one Val told me about. The one they call the Iceman."

"Val's expecting me, I take it?"

"My husband said you'd come one day. He said that there was no escaping from you. I thought he exaggerated but I guess I was wrong."

"Husband?" The Iceman was seldom taken by surprise but this surprised him. Covering her, he gripped her wrist and raised her left hand and stared at the ring.

Misty almost flinched at his touch. She half-expected his skin to be cold but his hand was as warm as hers. "Why are you so shocked?"

The Iceman let go and stepped to the window. Careful not to show himself, he closed the shades. The only source of light was the TV, its glare playing over Misty's upturned face. He admired how she was trying to be brave even though her eyes betrayed how scared she was. He admired, too, that she didn't scream or indulge in hysterics.

"You haven't answered me, Mr. Iceman."

"I never figured him for marriage. In Vegas he had a reputation as a ladies' man."

"He's told me all about his life there."

"He's told you too much."

"I love Val and he loves me," Misty declared. "Do you know what it is to love someone with all your heart and soul?"

The Iceman saw that she wasn't being sarcastic. He saw something else, too. In a rush of intuition he perceived her innocence, her sincerity, the sweetness of her personality. "I'll be damned."

"Excuse me?"

"A love like that is a luxury denied me," the Iceman said with real regret.

Misty struggled to stay calm. It was hard to do with the business end of the silencer trained on her. "It's only denied you if you let it. My mother likes to say that God made a mate for each of us. All we have to do is find them."

"Where's Val?" the Iceman gruffly demanded. He didn't care to be reminded of his perpetual loneliness.

"He went to see someone about our new driver's licenses and other papers. He didn't tell me who he was seeing or where it was."

The Iceman believed her. He debated whether to kill her or keep her alive on the off chance Val might phone and wonder why she didn't answer.

"I saw the news,"Misty mentioned. "All those people. Twenty-one men, women and children. How could you?"

"Twenty-three," the Iceman said.

"I saw about Mr. Johnson's little boy and little girl. Why did they have to die?"

"Sometimes kids hear their parents talk." The Iceman wasn't happy about having to do them but Franco wanted him to clean house. Their grandmother and her noisy dog he hadn't given a second thought.

"How did you find us?" Misty asked. She thought that if she could keep him talking, she could delay him shooting her.

"You have yourself to blame."

"Me? What did I do?"

"You called home yesterday morning," the Iceman said. "You told your mother where you were. You told her not to worry, and not to let anyone else know."

"How did---?" Misty began, and cold fear gripped her. Forgetting herself, she started to stand.

"Don't be stupid," the Iceman warned, and she sat back down."I planted a bug in their farmhouse, in the kitchen near the phone. After you called I paid them a visit." He glanced at the TV. "It must not be on the news yet."

"You killed my mom and dad?" Misty choked out. A swirl of emotion made her want to scream. She came up off the couch with her fingernails hooked to rake and scratch. She didn't care what happened. Two of the people she loved most in the world had been taken from her.

The Iceman hit her, a hard stroke across the temple that buckled her to the floor with her golden tresses framing her face like a halo. He put the silencer to her ear. "You shouldn't have done that," he said.

CHAPTER FORTY-FIVE

Val was pleased. Leski the Greek had come through. In his jacket were new lives for Misty and him. He could start over, free from the Thing.

A celebration was called for. Val stopped at a liquor store and bought a bottle of wine. He also picked up a bucket of chicken. He'd rather eat pasta---real pasta, not the can and frozen stuff---but he dared not visit an Italian restaurant. Eateries were favorite Mafia fronts, and L.A. Mafiosos were bound to be on the lookout for him. Big Frank would have sent word to all the Families.

The deaths of his friends had upset him tremendously. Cry Baby, he could understand. Lou's life for Scola's. But what had the others done to deserve being whacked? Switch, Pretty Boy, Dill and the Wolfman hadn't broken any of the rules.

Val realized that he owed his life to Misty. Falling in love, eloping, had saved him from a slug to the head. If he'd been at KLAS when the Iceman paid the station a visit, he'd be six feet under with the rest. He knew the chief enforcer did all the killing. Only someone of the Iceman's caliber could breeze in and out of Yuba City and leave so many bodies in his wake.

Val thought about Misty, lovely Misty, waiting alone in their cramped apartment. He vowed that before another week was out, they'd move. Before six months were out, he'd have the down payment for a home with a yard and a flower garden. Maybe it wouldn't be a mansion but it would be theirs.

Rounding the last corner, Val looked up at their window and noticed the shades were drawn. He walked briskly on and was almost to the stoop when it occurred to him that this was the first time the shades had been shut. Ordinarily, Misty was at the window, eagerly watching for him.

Inner alarm bells clanged.

Val pressed the button for 318 instead of 317. He'd run into the old lady who lived there a few times in the hall and when she came on, he explained who he was and that his arms were full of groceries and he'd pressed the wrong button. Would she please buzz him in?

Val padded up the stairs rather than take the rickety, and noisy, elevator. The stairwell door creaked but not loud enough to be heard in their apartment. The hallway was empty. He crept to their door, set the wine and the food down, and put an ear to it. The TV was on. He could hear a newscast.

Val wondered if he was overreacting. Maybe there was a simple explanation. Maybe Misty had closed the shades because the sun was in her eyes while she was watching TV.

Val raised a hand to knock, but didn't. It was better to be too cautious and breathing than not cautious enough and dead. Extracting the key from his pants pocket, he gingerly inserted it into the lock. He flinched when it scraped.

Staying clear of the doorway, Val palmed his pistol and slowly turned the knob. He risked a peek.

Misty was curled up on the couch on her side, apparently

asleep.

Grinning at his foolishness, Val shoved the pistol into his holster, retrieved their supper, and strolled in, saying as he kicked the door shut, "Rise and shine, wife of mine." He was only a few feet from the couch when he saw strips of towel around her wrists and ankles. She was unconscious, not asleep. He started to lower the bags but it was too late. A hard object was jammed against the nape of his neck.

"Don't so much as twitch," the Iceman warned.

Val turned to marble. He had no idea how the enforcer had found them. Nor did he care. Misty's life was the only thing that mattered. His own had been forfeit the day he took his oath of allegiance to the Mafia.

The Iceman slid his free hand under Valentino's jacket. He took Val's pistol and tucked it under his own belt, then patted him down. Only when the Iceman was satisfied there were no hideouts did he step back and say, "You can turn around if you want. I owe it to you to do it face to face."

Still holding the wine and the food, Val slowly turned. "Why the rest of the crew?"

"All the questions you could ask and you ask that?"

"It wasn't right."

The Iceman sidled next to the television. Leaning on it, his pistol trained on Val's chest, he frowned. "I agree. But it's not my place to refuse. When Franco says to do something, I do it. My personal feelings don't enter into it."

Val noticed a cut on the enforcer's neck and nodded at it. "Switch?"

"Good eyes. He damn near nailed me. If he'd been as good with a gun as he was with knives, I wouldn't be standing here. He was the fastest, ever."

Val was puzzled as to why the Iceman hadn't squeezed the trigger. One of the first lessons every soldier learned was that when someone had to be whacked, you walked up and whacked them. You didn't make small talk. He gauged the distance between them.

The Iceman made a tsk-tsk sound. "Don't insult me. You'll be dead before you take a step." He motioned at the bags. "What do you have there?"

Val told him.

"A bottle of wine? How about if you pour us each a glass? After, I'll do you and your sweetheart. I promise no pain. And I'll do you first so you don't have to watch her die."

"Why so nice?"

The Iceman didn't reply right away. Finally he said, "Would you believe that you were the only one in the Family to be friendly? The rest were too scared."

Val grasped at the straw. "Repay the favor." He jabbed an elbow toward Misty, who had groaned. "Let her go."

"Even if I wanted to, I can't," the Iceman said. "You told her about me, and probably about Franco. That makes her a threat to him, and that I can't allow."

On the couch, Misty heard herself groan. She seemed to be climbing toward a fuzzy light. She heard voices, too, one of them her husband's. Suddenly she remembered. Dread washed through her and she opened her eyes. Someone was standing in front of the couch, blocking her view. She realized it was Val.

"I guess I'll have that wine," he said.

"You do the honors," the Iceman said. "Do it slow and

keep your hands where I can see them."

Misty needed to let Val know she had come around. Easing her head off the couch, she rubbed her cheek against the back of his thigh.

Val nearly jumped out of his skin. As it was, he took a half-step and caught himself, bracing for a shot to the brain.

"Are you that anxious to die?" the Iceman asked.

"Sorry," Val said. "The bag was slipping. My hands are sweaty." That last was true. His face, too. He realized that the Iceman wasn't aware Misty had revived. It was smart of her to let him know the way she did. He wondered if he could count on her to do what needed doing.

"Put the bags on the table," the Iceman directed.

"Now?" Val said, saying it louder than was necessary in the hope Misty would understand.

The Iceman was amused. "Sometime today would be nice, yes. I have a flight to catch in a couple of hours."

The comment prompted Val to ask an important question. "Back to Vegas? What did Big Frank say when you told him where we were?"

"I haven't yet."

To Val that made no sense. "I should think he'd want to know."

"I figured I'd be sure you were still here and give him the good news when you're both taken care of." The Iceman gestured at the bags. "Do you want the wine or not?"

"Sure. Let me set these down now." Again Val said the last word louder than was called for, and when nothing happened, he repeated it louder yet. "Now!"

Misty was listening closely. When he said it the second time she'd guessed it was a signal. He wanted her to do something, but what? She was bound and helpless. Then he said it the third time, urgently, and she did the only thing she could think of. She heaved up onto her elbows and shrieked at the top of her lungs.

Not once in his long career had the Iceman ever given those he killed a break. Sparing Valentino, however briefly, was a weakness. He'd let himself grow fond of a fellow wiseguy. But he was no amateur. When Val said 'now' the second time, he was instantly wary. When Val said it yet again, even louder, he leveled his pistol. A scream and movement on the couch delayed his shot for a split-second.

He glanced over, saw it was only the girl, and focused on Valentino again.

That split-second was the distraction Val needed. He threw himself at the enforcer, the bags of food and wine between them, and seized the Iceman's wrist.

The silencer coughed and a slug thudded into a wall. They fell against the TV stand and the silencer chugged again, sending lead into the couch.

The Iceman's other hand clamped like a vise onto Val's wrist. Locked together, they struggled.

"Misty, get down!" Val shouted, afraid she'd be hit by a stray shot.

Iron resolve filled the Iceman. He tried to point the pistol but the bags were in the way. Furious at his own sloppiness, he sought to push the younger wiseguy away so he could get a clear shot.

Val clung to the Iceman for dear life. A knee exploded in his groin and he buckled, pulling the Iceman down with him. They rolled against the table, against the couch. The Iceman's forehead slammed into his jaw and the room burst into flashing pinpoints of light.

With a deft flip, the Iceman got Valentino under him. He slammed his knee into Val's gut and Val's grip weakened. Wrenching his arm free, the Iceman pressed the silencer to Val's forehead. "Thanks for reminding me there's no fool like a sentimental fool."

Misty was on her side on the couch, her knees tucked to her chest. She had drawn her legs up to make herself as small as possible in case the gun went off again. Now, seeing the man she loved imperiled, she thrust her feet straight out, into the Iceman's face. Cartilage crunched and his sunglasses nearly fell off.

The Iceman swung toward her and brought his pistol up and around.

That was when Val's vision cleared. He saw Misty about to be shot. He saw, too, his own pistol wedged under the enforcer's belt. Yanking it out, he shoved the muzzle into the Iceman's stomach and fired. Even partially muffled, the blast was a thunderclap.

Enzo was knocked back. He suddenly felt abominably weak. There was the blast of a second shot and his arms drooped. He looked down at a spreading crimson stain. He could feel his life force ebbing but he had enough strength left for one shot. He could still shoot Val or he could shoot the girl. He saw the look she gave Val and the look Val gave her---and he let his pistol drop to the floor and followed it down into a cold void.

Val pushed to his feet. He darted to the counter that served as their kitchen and snatched up a steak knife. A few strokes and Misty was clutching him.

"I was so scared."

Val wanted to soothe her, to smother her with kisses.

Instead, he pried her off and hustled her toward the door, grabbing her purse on the fly. "Half the people in the building must have heard those last shots. We've got to get out of here before the cops show up."

The corridor was empty. Bitter experience had taught the tenants that the better part of civic duty was to stay behind their doors.

Val held his pistol close to his side until they were at the bottom of the stairs. The street seemed normal. No one stared as they walked to the Neon. It had California plates Val had taken from another vehicle. They hurriedly climbed in.

Rubbing her wrists, Misty leaned back in the passenger seat. "What next? Where are we going?"

The anxiety in her voice prompted Val to gently grasp her hand and pull her over so he could kiss her. "Name it. Anywhere you want. Any state, any city."

"But the Mafia?"

"We're safe now," Val said. "The Iceman was the only one who knew where we were." He laughed for joy. With their new identities, they had a future.

"Safe," Misty repeated, smiling.

"Where do we start our new life?" Val asked.

Misty kissed him. "I hope you won't think this is silly but I've always had a hankering to see Nebraska. I hear tell the folks there are really nice."

"Whatever the lady wants, the lady gets." Val had driven through the Cornhusker State a few times. Flat came to mind, and cows. But who cared? He'd be happy so long as he was with her.

Misty nuzzled his neck. "I love you so much."

"I love you more."

Already, Val was looking ahead. Misty could get work as a secretary. As for him, he'd try various jobs until he found one he liked. And if he didn't find one, well, there were other ways to make money.

FINI

**Don't miss more geat reads by
David Robbins!**

ANGEL U
LET THERE BE LIGHT

Armageddon is a generation away. The forces of light and darkness are preparing to clash in the ultimate battle. To prepare humankind, the angels establish a university of literal higher learning here on Earth. A young man and a young woman meet, and begin to fall in love. Only to be caught up in demonic warfare when the ruler of Hell decides that Angel U must be destroyed at all costs.

ANGEL U
DEMIGOD

Gilgamesh the Destroyer. Demon Slayer. Giant. Son of the Moon. Seeker of Immortality. Two parts god, one part human. He wants nothing to do with the war between Heaven and Hell. Then Gilgamesh learns that he is not who he thought he was. He is not *what* he thought he was. To uncover the truth, Gilgamesh will venture where few have ever dared.

ENDWORLD #28
DARK DAYS

Apocalypse now. The science fiction series that sweeps readers into a terrifying future continues. The Warriors of Allpha Triad face their greatest threat yet. Their survivalist compound, the Home, has been invaded. Not by an enemy army. Not by the horrifying mutates. This time a shapeshifter is loose among the Family. Able to change into anyone at will, it is killing like there is no tomorrow.

ENDWORLD #29
THE LORDS OF KISMET

From out of the horror of World War III a new menace is spawned. Claiming to be the gods of old, their goal is global conquest. Enter the Warriors. Three are sent to bring the Lords down. But there is more to the creatures than anyone imagined, and before long a terrible truth dawns. Sometimes the good guys lose.

ENDWORLD #30
SYNTHEZOIDS

Three Warriors have been laid low. They can be saved. But only if another seasoned Warrior leads four green trainees into the heart of darkness and madness known as the Valley of Shadow. It is a run like no other, with more than lives hanging in the balance.

A GIRL, THE END OF THE WORLD AND EVERYTHING

Courtney Hewitt lived a perfectly ordinary life. Then several countries let fly with nuclear missiles and chemical and biological weapons and her life was no longer ordinary. Now Courtney has chemical clouds and radiation to deal with. To say nothing of the not-so-dead who eat the living. A lot of people might give up in despair. Not Courtney. When the going gets tough, the tough kick butt. (ENDWORLD fans! This an ENDWORLD prequel.)

BLOOD FEUD #2
HOUNDS OF HATE

Chace and Cassie Shannon are back. The feud between the Harkeys and the Shannons takes the twins from the hills of Arkansas to New Orleans, where Chace has a grand scheme to set them up in style. But if the Harkeys have anything to say about it, they'll be ripped to pieces.

THE WERELING

The original Horror classic. Ocean City has a lot going for it. Nice beaches. The boardwalk. Tourists. But something new is prowling Ocean City. Something that feasts on those tourists. Something that howls at the moon, and bullets can't stop. The Jersey Shore werewolf is loose.

WILDERNESS #67
THE GIFT

Evelyn King is sixteen and in love. She conspires to trick her parents and sneak away with the young warrior who has claimed her heart. Only they don't know that four killers are on the loose, slaughtering settlers and anyone else they come across.

WILDERNESS #68
SAVAGE HEARTS

Nate and Winona King thought they were doing the right thing when they rode deep into the Rockies to return a little girl to her people. Little did they realize: some good deeds are fraught with perils.

WILDERNESS #69
THE AVENGER

'Vengeance is mine', says the Lord. One man doesn't believe in that. He believes he has the right to slay the man who killed someone close to him. And he will move heaven and earth to do so. The man he is out to slay? Zach King.